FRIENDS OF THE DUKE
INCONVENIENT BRIDES PREQUEL ANTHOLOGY

NINA JARRETT

Babooks.

NINA JARRETT

$\mathcal{I}$nterview with the $\mathcal{D}$uke

INCONVENIENT BRIDES

PREQUEL

PROLOGUE

Oh, sweet sorrow to recall the blood one has lost.

A gust of wind grabbed hold of Lord John Pettigrew's beaver and flung it back before he could react. Spinning on his heel, he gave chase as it skittered down the street he had just exited. The hat had been a gift from his older brother, whom he had not seen in some time, and it was too valuable to him to allow it to escape. It came to a stop on the filthy London roadway, but John was determined as he grimaced at the unmentionable things that would need to be brushed—nay, scrubbed—off the expensive piece.

As he bent over to pick it up, a door opened nearby and a pair of polished Hessians stepped out of Hatchards bookshop and into his peripheral vision, causing him to stumble off-balance. A large, sun-bronzed hand shot out to steady him as John tried to find leverage while grabbing for the brim of the headpiece. The man holding him up was strong, preventing John from sprawling face-first in a ripe pile of horse manure currently gracing the dirty street cobbles.

Once he had regained his balance, John straightened,

much more gracefully than he had folded over, to thank the man for his hasty intervention.

"Pettigrew?"

John looked up into a familiar face. "Halmesbury! I mean … Your Grace." He sank into a bow.

The young duke snorted. "Don't be ridiculous, John. If you insist on 'your gracing' me, I will have no choice but to 'milord' you, so let us behave like old school chums who have just been reacquainted after some years apart, shall we?"

John smiled. Halmesbury was as modest as he remembered from their Oxford days, which was a pleasant discovery. Since his father had disinherited his own sorry arse, demonstrating implicitly that John was the unnecessary spare, many of the peers he had considered friends had shunned him. He no longer had a generous quarterly allowance; he was no longer connected to a marquess; and, horror of horrors, he now wrote for a living. Worse, *he made a living* instead of being an indolent second son living off his father's fortune.

"It is good to see you, Halmesbury. And thank you for catching me." John gestured at the offensive pile.

"What are you doing right now, Pettigrew? Do you have time to accompany me to a coffee shop so we can catch up?" the duke queried in his deep baritone as he released John to swipe errant blond strands from his own face. John's smile widened. The duke had always worn his hair a little long and was perpetually sweeping it back with his hand. Lord, it was good to see his broad, friendly face again.

"You drink coffee, Your Gr—Halmesbury?"

"Of course, Pettigrew, with a good book. I'm not much for the hard stuff, friend."

John smiled and nodded in agreement. They both turned in the same direction to make their way to the nearby coffee shop, clearly in one mind about the exceptional quality of that particular establishment.

* * *

WHILE JOHN SETTLED onto a crudely carved bench, the duke dropped down across the scarred tabletop onto his own bench. He topped John's five feet eleven by at least four or five extra inches, and he was broader of frame, so the seating was more awkward for Halmesbury. The duke took several moments to settle into a comfortable position.

"So tell me, John, why have I not seen you in so long? It must be four to five years since we last met?"

John's heart grew heavy in his chest as disappointment flooded him. Did the duke not know about his scandalous behavior? Would he see the man's expression grow cold when he explained his current circumstances? Pensively, he stared at Halmesbury for some moments, breathing in the aroma of roasted coffee beans and taking in the chatter of the other patrons.

"The marquess cut me off."

"What?" The duke looked flabbergasted. "Why would he do such a thing? You were always such a good … Why? When?"

"Back in 1814, he purchased me a commission. Unbeknownst to him, I had written a novel that had just been accepted by a publisher. When he told me of the commission, I informed him of my decision to pursue a career in writing, and we … had words." John winced at this understatement. More like a holy war that had raged for weeks as his father had flung accusations of cowardice and ingratitude, followed by tirades about not knowing one's place in the world—John severed the torturous thoughts. Even years later, the memories were still raw and painful. It was fortunate he had Dinah

Honeyfield in his life to sweeten his sentiments and relieve the pain of losing his family.

"A novel, you say?" To his surprise, the duke's expression reflected interest, not disdain.

"Yes. The marquess accused me of being a coward for shirking my duty and threw me out. I have been writing ever since." John added the extra information as if some compulsion drove him to challenge the duke to reject him. He preferred to not prolong their meeting and just reach the inevitable outcome quickly.

"Truly? What have you written?" The duke's interest did not appear to wane.

"A novel, two volumes of poetry, and I write articles for *The Gentleman's Magazine*."

Halmesbury looked astonished. "Incredible ... I never knew you had such an interest in writing."

"As the second son of an important noble, I was trying to learn my place. But I reached the day I could no longer deny my passion for the written word, and I had to pursue it."

The duke mulled on this, no sign of rejection or contempt yet evident. "That sounds like a terrible sacrifice to have made."

John struggled to follow his meaning. After a few seconds, he pointed to himself. "You mean *me*?"

The duke tilted his head in assent.

John bobbed his head in astonishment. "You think *I* sacrificed?"

"Of course. The easy path would have been to bow to your father's desires and take the commission you did not want, would it not? As the son of a marquess, you likely would have been assigned something in administration if you had wished it, thus never experiencing a moment of danger during your service."

John pondered his remarks. "Well, I don't know what to say. You are the first to view it that way."

The duke frowned in confusion. "What do you mean? How has it been viewed?"

"That I am a coward for not donning the scarlet coatee. That I was avoiding my duty. Not to mention the scandal of being engaged in a disreputable career and turning my back on centuries of noble tradition."

"Other members of polite society may not hold honest work in high esteem, but I do. And avoiding your duty was not the impetus for your decision, was it?"

"Well … no."

"Then, *pish*, art is important. It inspires men to dream, to aspire to new heights. Mayhap, to dream of new solutions that do not involve cutting men down in battle and leaving widows and orphans to fend for themselves. As I see it, you took a risk. You walked away from a life of certain luxury to forge your own path and do what was right for you. Are you a good writer? Do you have something meaningful to contribute?"

"I like to think so."

"Well, then, there you go. You are not a coward, but a brave man to face the unknown."

John stared at the duke for several seconds, steady gray eyes staring right back at him. They both lifted their coffees to take a sip and grimace at the bitter beverage. It was an acquired taste. By all appearances, Halmesbury was intimately acquainted with the intricacies of coffee-drinking. John dropped his gaze to stare down into his cup before raising his head to break the silence.

"And you, Halmesbury? What have you been up to?"

"I married—"

"Congratulations!"

"—and was widowed."

John winced. "Good Lord, I am so sorry, friend."

"So am I, Pettigrew, so am I. The duchess was a beautiful young woman and taken from the world far too soon."

"*Zooks!* Halmesbury, that is terrible. Losing my family left a hole in my soul, a metaphysical wound that will never fully heal. They are my blood … but it seems trivial compared to losing your wife … Hell, listen to me running off at the mouth! My apologies, Your Grace, and my condolences."

"Thank you and not at all. It is a pity—and unnecessary—that this happened to you, and I understand the desire to vent to an old friend."

"You were always a good listener, Halmesbury. I am glad to find you unchanged in that regard."

The duke's face fell for a moment, his eyes haunted as he looked away. "Would it be, friend, would it be."

John suppressed a shiver as his writer's eyes glimpsed into the other man's soul, straight to some undisclosed, festering wound. A moment later the duke smiled, composed once more, as if he had not a care in the world. John's heart squeezed to realize that his old friend was masking great pain and he, John, had not the means to alleviate it.

"Now, tell me, Pettigrew, how can I be of assistance?"

John's head bobbed up in surprise at the change in subject. "Truly?"

Halmesbury gave a nod.

"Well … I make my regular income from *The Gentleman's Magazine*. If you would grant me an interview—"

The duke winced. "Egads, John, anything but that! I hate being in the public eye! You know that … *damn* …" John stayed silent while the duke appeared to consider it. "All right, I will allow an interview, but the article will be about my philanthropic work, to promote charitable causes, mind you. That is the only subject I am willing to discuss in a publication."

John nodded as he reached into his burgundy tailcoat to pull out a fresh, leather-bound notebook and a graphite pencil. He had just purchased both the items at his favorite stationery shop that morning, which now turned out to be fortunate timing.

"Then tell me about this charitable work?"

"Let me see ... I guess it all began when my housekeeper, Mrs. Thorne, approached me to discuss the Halmesbury Home for Children ..."

* * *

IT WAS EARLY the following morning when John came to be seated across from his editor while the balding, old man scanned the pages covered in John's—admittedly untidy —scrawl.

Mr. White was a scrawny figure filled with nervous energy, who frequently sought his eyeglasses as he chewed on the end of a cheap cigar. The eyeglasses were usually clamped onto his head, resting on the top of his balding pate in a steely embrace, so John could not understand why the editor did not feel the tight grip of the arms pressing against his skull. He had diplomatically withheld the urge to point them out when the man had scurried around searching for them just moments ago because he had learned his lesson during their very first meeting, when Mr. White had been affronted by John pointing to his missing eyeglasses.

John now knew to never point them out unless specifically asked to by this cantankerous major of the magazine's writing troops.

Mr. White had finally discovered them and was currently reading the article John had prepared the day before.

"Halmesbury? The reclusive duke? How did you get an interview with him?" Mr. White's questions were tossed across the desk of haphazard papers and semi-organized chaos.

"I attended Oxford with him."

"Outstanding … but why this dissertation on the import of charitable works?"

"It was the only topic he was willing to discuss. He made some interesting points, and I believe our readers will be enthralled to hear from the duke in any capacity."

"True, true …" Mr. White finished skimming the pages and looked up, fixing his beady eyes on John. "This is good. I think we will print it in the August issue of *The Gentleman's Magazine*. The readers will eat it up. Well done, Pettigrew. I knew your connection to the peerage would eventually benefit our modest establishment."

John smiled in appreciation. Writing for a publication was not his first choice, and White was difficult to please, but the assignments provided him with a livelihood so he could continue to work on publishing his own words.

He anticipated that this unprecedented article with the notoriously private, but powerful, peer would garner positive attention for him as the author of the piece. If he played his cards right, it might lead to one day securing a wealthy patron, which would be very helpful for his future plans to woo the lovely Dinah Honeyfield. Encountering Halmesbury the day before had been a boon in more ways than one.

CHAPTER 1

Demented fool, lost in his thoughts;
worlds to explore, battles to be fought.

Miss Dinah Honeyfield was angry. Nay, not angry. *Very angry.* Not at her father, who had just informed her that they would soon be leaving for Bath on a husband hunt.

Nay, Dinah was not angry with Papa. She was angry with the procrastinating, infuriating, frustrating, confounding, charismatic, artistic, devastatingly handsome Lord John Pettigrew! This was *his* fault for not coming up to scratch. She *knew* he had feelings for her. He *must*! They spent all their time together, shared many interests, partook in lively debates, threw persistent longing glances at each other, and yet Papa's infernal houseguest never gave any indication that he would court her! Not one sign. Not in four long years. It was beyond the pale, and she was not going to allow it to continue one moment longer while her father dragged her cross-country to meet other, inferior men.

Dinah stormed into the library, banging the door open to find the reprobate sitting at his customary writing desk with a quill poised over paper. "John!"

His lean figure jerked in surprise as he turned to look at her. She stormed up to the desk to stand over him. Arms akimbo, she hoped she struck an intimidating pose. At an even five feet, it was hard to be taken seriously. She wished she had grown taller so she could face off more effectively with the idiot men in the Honeyfield household.

"My father is taking me to Bath to find a husband! What do you intend to do about it?"

John's narrow face blanched before he composed himself. "Do?"

"Don't you pretend you know not of what I speak, *Lord John Fitzgerald Pettigrew!*"

He winced when she clipped out his full name. Good. Now he knew he was in trouble.

"Dinah, calm yourself. Take a seat and explain what you want of me."

"No!" His eyes widened at her commanding tone.

"You will do something about this! About us!" Dinah grasped the lapel of his navy tailcoat and yanked him forward to plant a clumsy kiss on his firm, sculpted mouth. He froze, then grasped her by the forearms to set her back.

"Dinah, what is this? What are you doing?"

"I am declaring my intentions! I have waited four long years, and I will not wait four more seconds." She stepped forward to once again press her inexperienced lips against his. Fortunately, he was seated, so she could reach them. As she brought her hands up to his shoulders, she leaned into him. She had no idea what she was doing, but she liked the feel of his warm lips. Lips she had imagined touching with hers on a thousand restless nights, and it felt good to finally be—

John groaned before lifting his arms to embrace her, pulling her closer as his mouth moved against her own. She sighed in relief when she felt him respond, only to be startled a moment later when his velvety tongue dipped inside to explore her. She stopped breathing in delighted suspense before responding with ardor. His hands stroked down her back, awakening a trail of tingling sensation—

He suddenly wrenched back. "Dinah, stop!"

"Why? I have waited so long for this. You must talk with my father, declare your intentions, so we may finally be together."

John moved her firmly away before standing up to tower over her. He was so … so … *too damn tall*!

"I cannot."

"But why? We are meant to be together. You feel it, too. I know you do!"

"Dinah, I am a lowly writer who does not even own his own home. I live as a guest here in your father's house and work hard to save so that I may one day be a man of conse-quence. Currently I am not, and I do not have the means to support a wife and family."

Dinah's hopes rose. He *was* interested in courting her. This unseemly delay was about wealth and standing!

"John, I am the only child of a wealthy merchant. I am an heiress! Coin is not an obstacle to us being together. Papa adores you, and you are the second son of a marquess. Offer for me and he will agree, I am certain."

"No, Dinah."

"But why not? I do not care about money. I care about you, you stupid man. I would live on your writer's wages if needs must. Anything to be with you. We belong together, John—"

"Dinah, I said no." John's tone was steely and certain. Her rush of bravado that had led her to confront him in the library withered and slowly died away. It was the expression on his face. He was resolute in his denial, and he did not look like a man who could be persuaded to consider her proposal.

"I admire you, Dinah, but I have my pride. I cannot let my wife be responsible for my income. I must make my own way. Prove myself. If I don't, my fathe—I *must* make my own way."

"But, John, I … we …"

"I cannot bring you down in this world. I cannot be the man who lowered your station."

"It will be all right, J—"

"Dinah Honeyfield, don't make me spell this out."

"But—"

"Dinah, there is no *we*. I will not be a fortune hunter, so you will have to accompany your father to Bath, as he has planned." John gentled his tones, but the words stung nevertheless. Her heart cracked in her chest when she comprehended with dismay that John was refusing her advances. She had gambled her pride, her dignity, for nothing. Lord John Pettigrew had no intention of ever pursuing her because he wanted to earn the worthless respect from a father who did not even recognize him.

Tears pricked her eyes as she tried to think of what to say, but words would not come. He cared more about his hubris than he did about her. She turned away, seeking the door before she embarrassed herself further by weeping in front of the man she loved … who did not love her. At least … not enough.

God's mercy! Was there a dignified way to end the conversation, or should she just pick up her skirts and run?

Run! She stumbled toward the door as the tears welled up and flowed down her cheeks.

"Dinah!" He called out to her, but she did not respond. She needed to escape.

* * *

WHEN DINAH RUSHED OUT of the library in a flounce of ivory lace and skirts, John was left standing at his favorite writing desk in a mild state of shock, his heart racing with both unleashed excitement and guilt. He raised his fingers to where Dinah had pressed her lush, warm mouth against his. He had thought to never have an opportunity to kiss her rose-colored lips. Now his body was alight with fired passion as his glorious muse departed and shame assailed him for bringing her to tears.

He wished he could do as she asked. He had thought about offering for her a thousand times, but there were no circumstances in which it felt right. He was not penniless, but he did not have very much. He would have even less if not for the generosity of Mr. Honeyfield these past years, who had welcomed him as a houseguest after first reading John's works and meeting with him.

Little had either man realized that John would, in effect, take up permanent residence in the merchant's lavish Mayfair home. However, it was the only possible outcome after that first evening when he had been invited for dinner and a young Dinah Honeyfield had entered the room. He could only describe it as an attraction at first sight that had swiftly grown into admiration, then love.

A petite redhead with soulful gray eyes, fine features, and a fiery, humorous temperament, Dinah had quickly become his muse while inflaming his blood. She was a tidal wave, dragging him under with the power and force of her personality. He was fascinated, bewitched, and enslaved, which was why he had remained on in the Honeyfield home.

Now, somehow, four years had slipped by as John had enjoyed her company and restrained his passion. Apparently, Mr. Honeyfield had finally grown impatient with her lack of suitors, a situation of Dinah's own causation, because she likely discouraged any men who surely flocked to the feisty beauty. Taking her to Bath to hunt fresh grounds was an astute move by the crafty merchant, but for John it was devastating news. He had barely had time to process his shock before she had hurled herself into his arms and pressed her soft, plump lips to his. Lips he had dreamed about ravishing every night for years.

Now his beloved's luminous gray eyes were filled with tears that *he* had caused. *Hell, I have to set this right!* Their feelings for each other were now out in the open, and there could be no turning back. He would either have to find a way to offer for Dinah immediately, or he would be forced by the discomfiture between them to depart the Honeyfield home.

His heart felt heavy in his chest at the thought of leaving the Honeyfields. He knew he would regret every moment of every day for the rest of his life if he walked away without making an effort to win her.

Christ! There must be a way to move forward. He could no longer wait for the article on Halmesbury to be published. August was months away, and his hopes that it would provide an opportunity would not be realized soon enough to address the current situation. He needed to find a patron who would agree to a long-term commitment. And very soon. Immediately, in fact.

But he no longer had connections, and he did not have many published works to his name because he spent most of his time writing for *The Gentleman's Magazine*, which was his only regular income source. John shook his head in dismay at the thought of another man claiming Dinah in marriage before he could announce his intentions. There must be a way, or fate was a cruel mistress without mercy to have presented him with his heart's desire, only to hold her beyond his reach!

He racked his brain until an idea struck him. The solution seemed painfully obvious in retrospect. Mayhap he did have one connection he could approach?

CHAPTER 2

Tempest, sharpened voice, correcting course;
new explorations of character and choice.

The following afternoon, the duke's butler answered the door at Markham House. Once John had produced his calling card to the slim, older man with the unusually hoarse voice, the butler had inspected it carefully, bowed, and then left him standing alone in the hall. This was promising; it appeared Halmesbury had not left for his country seat to summer in Wiltshire but was still in residence in London, to John's great relief. It was as if fate was in his favor today.

Shortly, he was shown down a grand hall bedecked with oil paintings framed in ornate gilt, and then into the duke's study, where an eclectic collection of *objets d'art* was on display. It appeared that the Markham ancestors were well traveled, as he spied African masks among the books on the ample walnut shelving, along with French ormolu clocks and Italian marble statuary.

"Pettigrew, come in, friend! Have a seat, but I do not have

much time to talk as I have an important appointment I must leave for." The duke consulted a fine, gold pocket watch and then spoke with his butler about his arrangements.

John held his breath, hoping he could speak with Halmesbury, yet anxious about a possible delay and uneasy about asking the man for his help. His nerve might fail him if he was forced to wait. He could not believe his daring in paying this visit.

Finally, the duke turned back to him after dismissing the butler. "I think I can spare an hour before I must leave. Will that be sufficient?"

John's spirits rose. He gave a nod and walked forward to take his place on one of the plush, red-upholstered armchairs positioned before Halmesbury's elaborate mahogany desk. His eyes fell to three familiar leather-clad volumes stacked on the edge. It appeared that the duke had purchased his novel and poetry since they had last seen each other.

Halmesbury took his own seat as he followed the direction of John's eyes. "This is most fortuitous timing, old chap. I confess I went directly to Hatchards and ordered all your books when we parted ways at the coffee shop. I just completed the second volume of your poems."

"I see that," John replied.

"I can now confirm that you are a good writer. Nay, an *excellent* writer and exceptional poet!"

John averted his eyes in embarrassed silence. He was not accustomed to receiving unfettered admiration, but Halmesbury had always been a generous man, even in their youth.

"I thought about what you said, Pettigrew, as I read your words. You made the right decision when you followed your dreams, despite how difficult it may have made your life. The soul of an artist cannot cut men down in battle without leaving an indelible stain. If you had accepted the commission in 1814, you might have been shipped out to fight at

Waterloo in 1815 after Napoleon's escape. You could have been killed and then these words, these beautiful words, would never have been inked on paper so that I might one day sit here to read them. Nay, Pettigrew, the world is a better place because you did not don that soldier's uniform but, instead, pursued your dreams. That took courage, my friend, true courage."

The duke shook his head, as if considering troubled thoughts. "Even if you had survived the Hundred Days … you would have been a different man. A man who likely would have become blind to the beauty in this world and unable to describe it so that the rest of us could be reminded that this life is bigger than our troubles. I am grateful for the opportunity to have read these words and have been reminded that there is love in the world."

John cleared his throat in discomfort from such eloquent praise, equally astounded by the duke's accusation in regard to the content of his work. "Love?"

"The second volume is inspired by a muse, is it not? There must be a woman who has captured your imagination, Pettigrew?" Halmesbury picked up the second volume and turned to a page that he had marked to read out two lines.

"Locks of fiery sunset, strands of crashing waves,
A universe contained in every star-studded gaze."

The duke put the volume down to peer out the window for a moment as John sat in stunned silence and waited for Halmesbury to continue. None had previously noticed or commented on Dinah's influence on his work before. If Dinah herself had suspected it, she had been too modest to mention it. John had been careful not to allude to her, except in that one passage when he could no longer resist describing her, and he had thought most readers would not notice it as more than a metaphor for the subject of the poem. That the duke had picked it out of the entire volume … his perception was painfully astute.

"Those words, in particular, struck me. Your muse appears to be a lively young lady, which made me consider my future after too many gloomy, unchanging days of being locked in the past. It made me envision that one day I may encounter my own bold young woman who will coax me from this veil of relentless mourning in which I am entangled. I … I needed to read these words. They moved me … awakened me from dark dreams."

The duke hesitated, then cleared his throat. "I have not been moved in some time. What you write, Pettigrew, it is a gift. Do not doubt that. Your work is important, and you must continue to put quill to paper."

John was overwhelmed. All these years, he had hoped his work was meaningful, all the while suspecting it was frivolous. Fluff. That it made no difference. Hearing a lauded peer like the duke praise it … find meaning in it … to hear it had moved him … brought on a tide of unexpected emotion. Many moments ticked by while John waited for the lump in his throat to ease. He could not believe he had found the courage—nay, the audacity—to seek Halmesbury out today to put his request to him. It was gratifying to find the duke in such a receptive mood.

He thought of the hurt in Dinah's hopeful eyes, then dug deep to find the fortitude he needed to broach the reason for his visit.

"Well, on that note, I have a proposal," he finally ventured. The duke's face relaxed in obvious relief. Clearly the discussion had been awkward for him, too, and John was grateful that Halmesbury had taken the trouble to express his thoughts despite his obvious discomfort. The sentiments expressed were filling the dark places in John's soul with newfound confidence. He was on the path he was meant to follow, and the time for doubting himself was over. It was time to take his work seriously. Time to fulfill his destiny.

"I'm listening?"

John coughed into his clenched hand, took a deep breath, and leapt.

"I want to put a request to you—for your patronage of an important project. Something I have been planning for some months. You are familiar with *A Dictionary of the English Language* by the writer Samuel Johnson?"

The duke gave a nod.

"I aim to write a revised version. And just like Johnson, it will require a patron to provide funds and to lend their creditable reputation. It has been more than sixty years since his dictionary was published, and our culture has changed significantly in the interim. It is time to prepare a new dictionary––the language of *our* times––but like Johnson's work, it is not just an ordinary dictionary. It will be a literary work that will capture the very essence of our culture for generations to come. If I can do this work justice, people will read it centuries from today and understand what it was to live in this exceptional era, post-Napoleon, with a regent prince at the helm of our small kingdom during a time of unprecedented art and architectural awakening."

Halmesbury mused on John's words before finally speaking. "A new dictionary … I admit, I am intrigued. It has been some time, and if our fashions have altered so greatly in that time, it stands to reason that our language has transitioned considerably. What is your plan, exactly?"

* * *

By the time John left Markham House, he was walking on air. The duke had agreed to an annual patronage for the coming ten years to work on the dictionary, along with a promise to continue his patronage beyond that if John continued to present him with worthy projects. Halmesbury had extended the time period John had initially requested, as the gentleman insisted his poetry and novels must continue to be written concurrently.

The patronage would provide John with steady income in excess of what he could possibly hope to earn working piece-meal for *The Gentleman's Magazine*. He would now truly write for his profession and, more importantly, he could support a wife and family.

John anticipated offering for Dinah's hand, and his heart swelled with elation. His chance meeting with the duke was proving to be an impetus to great things. Increasing his speed, he hurried down the roadway to find his love and tell her the delightful news. Nothing could possibly bring him down. He was to live the life he loved, with the woman he loved. Paradise was at hand. His tempestuous, soon-to-be intended would be his, her lively spirit safe within their marriage as he allowed her the freedom to be herself. Another man would attempt to cage her, to tame her fiery spirit, but not he. Dinah was special, and he would be able to protect her because he was the man who loved her just as she was.

He still could not believe that his bald-faced temerity in approaching the duke had paid off, that he had taken fate into his hands to shape his own destiny. It felt good; he had never felt so alive as he did in this moment with self-assurance lightening his step. Dinah's courage in declaring herself had inspired him with the determination he needed, and now it was time to tell her the good news and hope it would return her good spirits.

* * *

DINAH SAT IN THE LIBRARY, pondering what to do about Lord John Pettigrew. From the moment she had first laid eyes on him at her father's dinner table, her life had finally made sense. She was born to meet John, marry him, and build a life with him. He gave meaning to her existence. He made sense of her hopes and dreams and stirred her to achieve new heights of intellect and thought.

Except, somehow, the future she had envisioned in that moment, her very life unfolding before her, had never quite begun. She spent all her time with the infuriating man. They spoke on everything; she helped him plot his articles and discussed his ideas with him before he set them to paper. She encouraged him when he doubted himself and sought him out to allay her own worries.

How could they not be meant to be together, to wed? How was it possible? What kind of universe would place her perfect mate in front of her, only to hold him beyond her reach? It was too much to bear. A tear slipped down her cheek as she sat at his favorite writing desk, his published works beneath her resting hand.

Perhaps if she had more time, she could browbeat him into talking to her father now that she had confirmed he harbored feelings for her in return. But there was no time. Her father was hell-bent on leaving for Bath within a few days, and the household had already begun preparations. Trunks were being brought from the attic, and some of the less used rooms even now had furniture festooned with white dust sheets to form ghostly figures, which reflected her recent gloomy mood precisely. It felt like time was racing away from her and there was naught she could do to deter its relentless and hasty march forward. Soon she would be parted from John, and she knew not how long her father would insist on touring the realm on his quest for a de facto heir.

She loved her only parent, but he could be so bloody-minded when it came to wealth and connections. His legacy, as he put it. He would be gravely disappointed by their expedition, for she planned to be at least as bloody-minded as he. *More. I plan to be more bloody-minded than he!*

However, in this moment, as she contemplated departing London and leaving John behind, Dinah knew she was growing desperate. Desperation which clouded her thoughts and gave her no room to breathe as she imagined that the clock across the room was gathering speed to tick faster and faster in time with her racing heart. She drew a shaky breath to calm her nerves. There had to be a solution to their situation, but the despair and the lack of time at hand kept her from—

"Dinah?"

She looked up to find John at the door. Tall, handsome, his dark locks disheveled as if he had been caught in a gust of wind. He lifted a hand to brush through his ruffled hair, but his curls had a mind of their own and bounced back to their unruly state, rejecting the serious expression on his lean face. She smiled in painful whimsy before dropping her eyes back to her hand extended on his published works.

"I have news, sweet Dinah."

She looked back at him as he crossed the room and dropped to one knee to peer directly into her eyes, his own a bright-eyed hazel edged with luxurious, sooty lashes that usually stirred her with envy, but not today.

"What is it?" She could hear the despondent tone in her voice, but could find no energy to alter it.

"Is your father here?"

"He is not. He went to dinner at the Montagues'. I pleaded a headache and stayed at home. I ... I do not feel sociable at the moment."

John lifted her hand from the books. Placing a fleeting

kiss on her fingers, he stood and gently drew her up. "Dinah, I have been a coward. I should have sought a solution to our circumstances long before today. My love, you are my very reason for breathing. You are in my thoughts every moment of every day. You are sunlight on a rainy day, yet gentle rain to ease my soul when troubles rage inside me. You are everything to me."

Dropping back to his knee, he raised her hand to hold it against his shaven cheek. Looking deep into her eyes, he continued. "If I were to approach your father for the honor of your hand, would that please you?"

Dinah's jaw dropped. "What? I thought you said … Did something … Are you toying with … What is this, John?"

"I had a meeting this afternoon, and I have procured a patron. I shall have a regular annual income to pursue my writing projects. I no longer need to write articles for *The Gentleman's Magazine*, but, more importantly, I will have the funds to establish my own household. In light of which, would you consider doing me the great honor of consenting to be my bride, sweet Dinah?"

Dinah clasped a hand over her mouth, surprise robbing her of words. "I … I …"

With that, she reached forward to grab him by the lapels once more and planted a clumsy kiss on his lips. "*Zooks!* Pettigrew, you infuriating man, show me how to kiss properly!"

John barked a laugh in response as he stood up. Wrapping his arms around her, he cradled her head in his large hand as he lowered his lips to hers.

CHAPTER 3

At last, honeyed lips and sighs of pleasure

As John lowered his head to capture Dinah's soft lips, he was overcome with a sense of bliss. He could never want for anything again. Everything he had ever dreamed of was now at hand.

A fleeting worry crossed his mind that life could not possibly be this easy, but when his lips touched hers, all thoughts were forgotten as sensation rushed through his body. She tasted sweet, and she smelled divine. He could not help stealing his tongue into her mouth. Dinah moaned, shooting sparks straight to his groin as he deepened their kiss.

His hands found their way to her waist as he brought her womanly form against his hardening body, his passion escalating when he felt her small, round breasts press against him through layers of clothing ... altogether too much clothing. As she moaned and arched into him with passionate fervor, he wondered how long Mr. Honeyfield would prolong the betrothal before John could at last make Dinah his wife.

After several blissful moments, he eased her away before their passions could get out of hand, stepping back to cool his lust. Dinah mumbled in befuddled protest and reached out to grab him back. And, God help him, he let her as his lips found hers once more before trailing kisses along her delicate jaw, down her slim neck to graze his teeth over the pulse at the base, beating like a drum, before licking to assuage her delicate skin. Dinah moaned in ecstasy as she arched with urgency into his body, her entire delectable form pressed against him. He groaned his approval as his blood fired even hotter at the signs of her arousal.

Realizing their kiss was blazing out of control, he once more stepped back, which startled Dinah into opening her passion-glazed eyes and once more stretching out her hands to grasp him.

"Dinah, love, we need to calm ourselves before this goes any further. I will approach your father in the morning, and then we can marry within a couple of weeks. It is not long to wait—"

"Why?"

"Why what?"

"Why do we have to wait?"

"Dinah, you are a gently bred woman, and I would not do anything to offend—"

"John, we are to wed soon. We are both quite aware that once a couple becomes formally betrothed, many take liberties before the wedding night."

"We are not formally betrothed."

"But we will be. You know my father likes you. You now have an income, and he will be tickled to be connected to a marquess. We have already waited for years to come together. Why should we wait any longer?"

John had to admit that his body was singing its complete agreement with Dinah's logic. The matter was practically a *fait accompli*, and his siren was arguing to enter his bed with him tonight. Why would he deny him--her--them?

His thoughts were confused, and the overriding need was to take what she offered. They would marry soon. He could not think of a single reason to counter her argument, not a single sound reason to wait.

You are a gentleman. You must refuse. Reluctantly, he agreed with his conscience. They could be married within two weeks; he needed to practice patience.

"Nay, my love, I must obtain your father's consent. I will speak with him in the morning."

Dinah pouted. "Do you have to be such a gentleman?"

He laughed as he gently set her back. "Is that not one of the reasons you love me?"

She huffed. "I suppose. That and your infallible logic are another reason. Primarily, though, I am in love with your handsome countenance and your gift with words, although *that* is not currently being demonstrated."

"You are arguing that if I was less handsome, you would not love me?"

Dinah thought about it. "Nay, you are very handsome. I would still love you if you were less handsome because even then you would be handsome, still."

John colored, pleased at her compliment, as he had always considered her the most beautiful woman he had ever beheld. "Thank you, vixen. With such pretty words, I feel compelled to provide you with kissing lessons."

With that he pulled her back into his arms, his blood singing with restrained lust as his lips found hers once more.

* * *

DINAH HAD EXPECTED that kissing John would be pleasant. She had not expected fire, thunder, lightning hitting the earth as her blood heated to a deep, throbbing desire for more, more, more of these startling sensations that swept through her body.

Understandably, she was indignant when he had brought their interlude to a halt.

They had enjoyed an appealing dinner in the dining room and both adjourned to bed early, but Dinah was afire and she would not let matters stand, which was why at about midnight, after she had heard her father arrive home and enter his bedchamber for the evening, she was scurrying in her night rail in the dark. She stubbed a toe on a table leg when she entered the hall of guest chambers in the far wing of the house. Hopping on one foot on the carpeted floor, she winced and grimaced but did not allow herself to whimper or curse as the sharp, shooting pain caused her to see spots while she clutched her injured appendage. Or she was sure it would have made her see spots if it had not been so damn dark, except for a solitary ray of moonlight shining through the windowpanes at the far end of the corridor.

Once she had caught her breath and was able to gingerly take a step on the injured foot, she once again hurried—limped—down to the last door on the right, which she believed to be the room that John occupied. She had never visited him in this wing of the house because it would have been utterly ruinous, but tonight she was willing to take the risk. Tentatively she gave a low rap, mindful of any footmen who might be about.

She heard footfalls crossing to the threshold, to her great relief, and pinned a smile on her face to greet him when he opened the door.

"Rogers, I said I am good for toni—Dinah!" John rasped in surprise before swiveling his head to check for servants. Grasping her by the arm, he tugged her into his room and swiftly shut the door. "What are you doing here?"

"I decided four years was long enough to wait. I want you to make me your wife tonight."

"My wife? We don't have a license and it is midnight—" Dinah arched an eyebrow provocatively. "Oh, you mean to *make* you my wife." She waggled her eyebrows in assent.

"We discussed this earlier, and we agreed I would speak with your father first."

"No, you decided, but I did not." Dinah lunged up to peck a clumsy kiss, missing his exquisite mouth and landing her lips awkwardly on his chin. To her ire, John swallowed a snorting laugh at her antics. *This is so unfair!* She was going to get better at it.

"Dinah, if your father finds us—"

"He will force us to marry. Problem solved." Enough talk. She felt silly with her mouth pressed against his chin, even if he did feel and smell divine. Traces of port, coffee, and the scent of a masculine soap. *Don't get distracted, you flibbertigibbet!* In a flash, she turned her head to fasten her lips to his. He drew a startled breath, but a moment later he responded, nudging her back against the door to take her lips in an expert, deep kiss. She moaned her desire while her blood fired, nearly swooning with ecstasy when his velvety tongue once more stole past her lips to entangle with hers. Hungrily, she kissed back, mimicking his overtures and running her hands up his muscular chest, up his shoulders, and into his dark locks. They were as soft as she had always imagined, and her excitement mounted as she pressed into him.

He drew back to mutter, "Easy, vixen. This will be better for you if we take our time."

Yes! At last he is allowing it to happen! She slowly combed her fingers through his silky hair, delighted when he groaned and captured her lips once more. His hands stole around her waist and caressed her gently through the thin fabric, sending heat to settle between her thighs. Slowly, he slid his hands down to cup her buttocks, and she stopped breathing for a moment in bliss as he fondled her.

"Dinah, sweet redheaded temptress, I have dreamed of you every night ..."

She shivered as he whispered against her cheek and ran his tongue down her neck to lick at the pulse racing at the base of her throat. Her head fell back against the door when his head dipped lower, and he fastened his lips on a pebbled nipple visible through her rail. She gasped, jumping in surprise but tugging his head closer as the sensation rocked through to her very core.

He grasped and lifted her, holding her between his body and the door, her rail riding up as she clasped her legs around his waist. They groaned in unison when his hard length made contact with her melting center, their lips locking once more while he rocked his hips into hers in a delicious rhythm that left her gasping for breath as he pressed his face into the side of her neck. Hearing his breathing had grown labored, her pulse increased in response. He brought up a hand to lift a lock of her unfash-ionable fiery hair to his face, breathing in deeply. "God, you smell sweet, vixen."

She moaned. "Only a vixen in your arms, my lord, because you drive me wild with passion ..."

"Oh, Dinah, so many nights ..." He lifted her in his arms, brushing his lips to her temple as he carried her across the room to lower her onto the counterpane of his bed. Leaning over her, he fanned her hair out to frame her face while he suckled and nipped her lips. It shocked her, but she leaned up to get closer as he continued to kiss her while his hand found her ankle and slowly trailed up her calf, dragging the thin rail along. He stopped to caress behind her knee, exploring the sensitive area with his fingertips before brushing his hand up her inner thigh and resting it close to her molten center where she craved his touch. He raised his head to stare into her eyes, his multi-hued hazel irises vivid in the candlelight. "Are you sure, my love?"

She gazed deep into his eyes, breathed deeply, and gave a slow, deliberate nod. "I've never been so sure about anything, John," she whispered and noticed with satisfaction how her words caused him to shiver. Then a troubling thought crossed her mind. "Have there been … other women?"

His gaze did not falter. "Not since I met you, Dinah. It's been a long four years, my love, pining for you alone."

Dinah's heart burst with joy. She growled fiercely as she raised her face to kiss him once more. With that encouragement, she felt his hand move to pull the rail up over her hips, which she lifted to assist him, and over her head.

Then … then she lay naked before him.

His eyes glazed as he took in her breasts, her thighs, and she felt a blush blooming over her skin, but she steeled her nerves not to move to cover herself. He groaned, his gaze locked on her exposed body while he lifted himself off the bed, whipping his shirt up and throwing it to the side so his chest was bared. Her eyes hungrily slid over his muscled shoulders, his defined chest with a light dusting of dark fur, and his flat nipples, to travel down to his sculpted abdomen cast with shadows. A rush of aching desire raced through her to pool between her legs.

His hands went to the falls of his trousers where he started to unhook the buttons. She could make out the straining front of his placket, and her eyes riveted with fascination as he slipped his trousers and small clothes down over his hips and to the floor, stepping out of them to kick them away. Her mouth fell open as she took in his swollen … swollen … swollen … *Blast, what does one call it? Manhood, mayhap?*

Dinah hated being in the dark, uninformed, but the books

she had managed to locate on this particular subject had been vague. Perhaps she should … perhaps she should pay attention to John's powerful, naked body over hers instead of letting her thoughts ramble about to consider word choices. *Yes, that is a much better idea.* She sat up as he moved toward her, pulling herself over the counterpane to wiggle underneath into the cool sheets. John grabbed the edge of the brocade counterpane and hastily drew it off to the other side of the mattress. His lean body met hers and it was heavenly. Dinah hissed at the contact of bare skin as he leaned over to take her lips in another deep kiss, his hand coming up to caress her bared breast, spreading warm sensation as she trembled with desire. His head lowered as he raised the plump mound of her breast to flick her turgid nipple with his hot, velvety tongue, again causing her to gasp and moan while she writhed closer. He trailed kisses over to the other side and swirled his tongue over her neglected areola as her blood heated in response.

John's hand glided from her bosom to trail down over her quivering abdomen, coming to rest on her lower belly while he toyed with the red curls shielding her … her … her … *damnit … womanhood,* perhaps? How was a virtuous woman meant to know how to communicate about … about … carnal relations? Dinah brushed her vocabulary frustrations aside when the most delicious sensation hit her as John's hands dipped between her thighs to find a central pleasure spot, her head falling back as she arched up and keened in startled delight. *Sweet Banbury cakes! That feels amazing—nay, transcendent—wonder—*Words failed her altogether as he brushed the tip of his finger back and forth over the sensitive spot, raising unimaginable sensations. Her desire grew, winding and coiling its way from her belly until it swelled in a startling crescendo while she helplessly writhed under his glorious, talented hand. Soon she was crying out in wrenching pleasure with John's lips descending on hers to muffle her screams as she hit the peak of brilliant sensation. Slowly, she fell back to earth to find herself panting with exertion.

"Watching you in crisis, oh my God, sweet vixen ..." John growled in her hair before nudging a knee between her nerveless legs. He positioned himself over her, and she felt his swollen *appendage—manhood—Not again, Dinah, stay in the moment, you empty-headed ninny—*brush against her slick entrance. This was it! John was going to make her his woman, and there would be no turning back—

"Dinah, this may be uncomfortable the first time. I have done what I can to prepare you, but there is no way to know—"

"John, do it! I want to feel you."

He stilled, then guided his *whatnot* as he pressed into her channel slowly. She felt a pinching sensation, but then he was inside her, filling with his large ... large ... large ... *thingummy*, slowly stretching her as her intimate muscles grew accustomed to taking his length.

Quickly, her passion reawakened, and she felt her channel clench at his *thingumbob*, her womanly body craving his invasion. John groaned as he seated himself inside her, sweat glistening on his forehead, and she was gratified to see how enthralled he appeared to be by their conjugal relations. Her eyes widened as he began to move, stroking back and forth with intimate tenderness; her desire rose back up to fever pitch as she clutched him and wailed her lustful agreement. *Good Lord, it feels good!* Did this make her wanton? She did not care, she could only ... feel. A second wave of ecstasy hit her as she smothered her face in his shoulder to swallow her keening. She felt her intimate muscles clenching at his *stick* tightly as he shuddered above her, groaning loudly as she felt him release in a hot rush inside her.

John collapsed over her, leaning on his elbows, his breathing ragged. He leaned down to kiss her mouth fiercely before retreating to rest on his side next to her. Several moments passed while they both recovered their breath.

"Are you all right, my love?"

"More all right than I have ever been," she replied as she rolled onto her side to run a questing hand over his chest and abdomen, sliding around to caress his firm buttock.

He smiled down at her and pressed another lingering kiss to her mouth, then rolled off the bed. She watched him as he crossed the room to the jug and washbasin. Dampening a towel, he returned to the bed while Dinah watched in fascination. His *manhood* had receded but was still a sight to behold as he leaned down and carefully washed her inner thighs. "I will have to disappear this towel and mayhap the sheets, too."

Dinah looked down at his hand, confused, until she caught sight of the bloodied towel. "Oh!"

"Do not worry, the evidence will disappear before morning, even if I have to start a fire to burn them. Or perhaps I will cut myself, which may be easier than explaining the missing linens."

She smiled and stretched, feeling satisfied she had finally claimed her man … or had her man claimed her? Whichever it was, it felt like a great journey had been completed and she was finally exactly where she was meant to be. In John's bed and, as soon as he spoke with her father, she would be by his side as they built their new life together. It was heaven.

CHAPTER 4

Two hours later, Dinah slipped from his bed. She gathered her night rail and pulled it over her head before standing by the bed to watch John breathing evenly as he slept. Her beloved man looked so young and vulnerable in his sleep. He would speak with her father in a few hours and then, hopefully, by the end of the day they could begin planning the arrangements to be wed.

It was fate. Destiny. And John had moved mountains to bring it to fruition. She loved him with all her heart, and she loved the night they had just spent in each other's arms. Leaning down, she pressed a light kiss to the crown of his head, his dark locks tickling her nose as she drew in his masculine scent.

"You are going?" John had opened one eye to look up at her. "I should escort you back." He began to sit up.

Dinah pressed him back down into the sheets. "Nay, it

will increase the probability of us being caught together, and I want your meeting with my father to be as painless as possible. Catching the two of us together in the hall will not set the right tone for your meeting. I can say I was looking for a book, or fetching something to eat from the kitchen, if I am discovered on my own."

He reached out and caught her hand, bringing it up to his lips to kiss her lightly on the fingers. "I love you, sweet vixen. I would do anything for you."

"I know." She smiled as she drew her hand away. "Dream of me, John."

"I will. Again." His voice floated behind her as she exited the room and gently shut the door. She found herself alone in the dark once more, and a shiver of trepidation ran down her spine. *Don't be a ninny, everything is going exactly as it should.* With that thought, she carefully made her way in the dark, determined not to stub her toes on the journey back.

* * *

JOHN TUGGED at his stiff collar, then fiddled with his cravat. It surprised him how nervous he was, lifting his hand to tap his knuckles on the study door. *Honeyfield is your friend. He will be delighted to welcome you into his family.*

Despite the assurance, his nerves climbed unabated.

"Yes?" Honeyfield called out. Opening the door, John entered the room.

Dinah's father was a short, wide man with a balding pate and a fringe of ginger hair streaked with gray strands. He had thick whiskers and looked very much like a jolly red walrus, with his determined gray eyes so reminiscent of his daughter. John was fond of the older man who had invited him into his home, and they often enjoyed conversations about books and poetry over a single glass of port in the evenings. The man was more encouraging, not to mention more pleasant, than his own father, and he advised John on his career from time to time, such as an uncle or fatherly figure might. John felt relatively confident approaching him to discuss a courtship with Dinah, although having debauched the man's only child the night before was perhaps not the best method to heighten his confidence as he felt guilt twisting his stomach into knots.

"Mr. Honeyfield, do you have a few moments?"

Honeyfield raised a bushy, red eyebrow and gestured to the seat in front of his desk. "So early in the day, John? Is it something serious?"

John's palms were sweating as he took the offered seat. "I have news I wanted to share. Yesterday I procured a patron for my dictionary, the one we have been discussing. The Duke of Halmesbury has agreed to a long-term relationship and an annual patronage, so I will no longer need to write for *The Gentleman's Magazine* but can focus on my own work."

Honeyfield's wide face split into a grin. "That is excellent. Such a distinguished connection. I was not aware you knew the duke?"

"We were at Oxford at the same time. He loves my work. His support will mean a significant change in my circumstances. I am quite pleased. He is a distinguished and highly respected man, which will lend considerable credibility to the project itself."

"Most assuredly, this is quite a triumph. Well done, young man."

"In light of which, I ..." John swallowed and then blurted out, "I wanted to ask your permission to court Miss Honeyfield."

Honeyfield's face immediately fell into a stern expression. John stopped breathing as he waited for the man to respond, but a sense of foreboding washed over him to see his host grow so solemn. Had he misjudged his relationship with the older man? Honeyfield had seemed quite keen on his career and took an interest in him personally. What would cause such a poor reception to his request?

"That will not be possible."

John's fingertips felt numb where they rested on his knees, and he was sure the blood had run out of his face to leave him pale and shaking. This meeting was swiftly turning into a disaster, and his thoughts raced as he tried to discern what mistake he had made. Dinah would be ruined if he did not handle this matter correctly. If they did not wed, it would force her to remain on the shelf as a spinster to hide their ill-timed night together. Not daring to display any of the panic sweeping through his form, he tried to think of what to say next.

"Sir, could I press you for a reason?"

"I'm sorry, son. I like you, and I think you have an exceptional talent, but you have no connections, no experience with business or money. Dinah will inherit an empire, and she will need a husband who can take care of her interests in an effective manner."

"I do have a connection to the duke. And he offered the services of his man of business to help me manage my income and to guide me on investments. Dinah's welfare would be my priority!" His voice had risen slightly as he spoke, and his cheeks felt flushed, so he drew a breath to calm the desperation mounting up within him. Dinah was relying on him, and he must seek a positive outcome to his meeting with Honeyfield.

"I'm sorry, son, but it is not possible. If you were still in touch with the marquess, I might have considered it, but *Dinah*—Miss Honeyfield to you—is my only child and I must do what is right for her and my future grandchildren."

John's mind scrambled for a rebuttal. "I apologize, sir, for being too forward. In regard to the marquisate, my older brother will inherit from the marquess. He and I are on excellent terms. If I talked with him and got a future commitment to reinstate the family connection—"

"John, your father is in excellent health and only in his fifties, so he could easily be with us for three decades yet. Nay, a promise from your brother for far into the future is not comparable to current connections that could guide you."

"But, sir, I have attended Oxford and I am a man of letters. I could learn from you and ensure your vision continues."

Honeyfield's usually cheerful countenance grew cold. When he spoke next, it was clear that he had grown angry. "It is not my responsibility to do so. You are not a suitor that I can consider. Dinah and I will leave on our tour, and we will seek someone suitable with the requisite connections and experience. Someone who can take care of her and protect her interests."

John's desperation reached a fever pitch, his cravat tightening around his neck as if it were a noose intent on strangling him. He thought of being separated from his heart and the consequences of their previous night together. Even now Dinah could be with child. He must persuade Honeyfield, no matter how awkward or uncomfortable this discussion was.

"Dinah has expressed her desire to receive my courtship—"

Honeyfield hopped to his feet, looking more like an irate Irish leprechaun in his green tailcoat than a jovial walrus as he thundered, "*Miss Honeyfield* will get over it. What right have you to call my daughter by her Christian name, Pettigrew? You, young man, have crossed a line. I think it will be best when we return from our tour that you no longer reside in my home."

John blinked, then attempted to placate the angry father. "Yes, sir, I had intended to establish my own household and investments. I … What would I need to change about my circumstances for you to consider my suit?" John was out of ideas and ill-prepared for such a chilly reception from the man he had considered his close friend. For Dinah, he must find a solution, or he would be the worst sort of scoundrel to have bedded her and then stand by as she was forced to depart with her father. Given her lack of virtue this morning, she would have to avoid any serious suit to hide the fact that she was now, by society's standards, a fallen woman. And he would be the man responsible for ruining a young woman's future. His blood pounded in his ears as he waited for Honeyfield to respond.

"I'm sorry, son. I Iike you, but without your connection to the marquess, you are no one of consequence … and my daughter … she is everything to me, my legacy, and she is a wealthy heiress who needs a proper husband of importance. You will recover if you have developed feelings for her because you are still young. And so will she. She is too young to know what she needs, which is why as her father I must make this difficult decision."

John once more felt robbed of breath as the man he considered a confidant echoed the accusations of his own father years earlier. That his desires were inconsequential, that *he* was inconsequential, that Dinah did not know her mind because she was too young. The ground seemed to shift beneath him when he came to the realization that he was failing Dinah because he had no arguments left. Perhaps if he had prepared better for this meeting, or had more time to broach the subject, to plan it out, but he had never considered that Honeyfield would find him unsuitable. To make matters worse, Honeyfield's harsh words confirmed all his worst thoughts about himself, and he felt his confidence plummeting as he considered his *lack of consequence*, as the merchant had put it.

"I … I see." John was desperate to change the outcome of the meeting to a maybe, instead of the resolute no he currently faced. Panic coiled in his gut while he frantically sought some method to convince Dinah's father to reconsider.

"May I reapproach you if I have a change of circumstances?" He had no concept of what that change could be, but it would at least buy him a second conversation.

"Pettigrew, other than reconciling with your father, what could possibly occur that would create a meaningful difference to what we have discussed? Nay, this is not a match that is meant to be." The older man's face softened. "There will be other women more suitable to your circumstances."

John bit back a retort. There had been no other women since he had met Dinah, and there would be none after. He had no choice but to change her father's mind, but at this moment his priority was to maintain civility so he could leave a door—or, more accurately, a very small window—cracked open that he may climb through it to speak with Honeyfield again. If he could think up any ideas with which to persuade him. For a man of words, he suddenly found himself with none to call on.

Perhaps he would follow them on the tour and wear the man down? No, that seemed unlikely. Honeyfield was as obstinate as his fiery princess.

Nevertheless, leave a small window cracked open, John! You will find a way, because you have no choice!

John rose. "I will find a way to change your mind, to be worthy of Dinah in your eyes. The next time we talk, you will accept my suit, Mr. Honeyfield, because Miss Honeyfield is incomparable. She cannot be replaced or forgotten, and I will find a way to inspire your confidence, sir!"

Honeyfield retook his seat. "Good day, Pettigrew."

CHAPTER 5

Iron wills, and clashing might;
no resolution to be seen in sight

*D*inah looked up as John walked into the library, closing the door behind him. Noting his gray pallor, her heart plummeted. Her father had declined. Why would he decline? He loved John. What reason would he have to reject the young lord's suit?

John walked over and dropped onto the other end of the sofa, pulling at his cravat to loosen it and undoing the top button of his starched shirt. He looked ill, and Dinah found her breath quickening as her heart raced with anxiety.

"What happened?"

"He was quite upset that I sought to court you. Apparently, I am a man of no consequence."

"What? That is an awful thing to say to you. Of course you have consequence. Do you think I would love a man who did not matter? Have you met me? I have impossibly high standards, which can only mean that you are of high consequence. And the Duke of Halmesbury happens to agree with me."

John gave a reluctant smile, but his expression remained stark. Dinah feared her father had made her beloved truly doubt himself after all her efforts to bring him up to scratch. She was angry again, but this time it was directed at her father.

"No matter. I shall pack a bag and we will be on our way." She was proud of how matter-of-fact she sounded when inside she quaked at the risk.

John scowled in confusion. "On our way?"

"To Gretna Green. To elope. My father does not get to decide whom I marry, and now that you have an income, we shall make our own way in the world without him."

"Dinah … I could never do that to you. The scandal … you would be ruined—shunned by all good society. Forever. I could never be responsible for such an outcome. I must find a way to change your father's mind."

Dinah snorted, rather inelegantly. "Change my father's mind? Are you insane? He never changes his mind. There are many men who have attempted to change his mind and failed. He has been responsible for men losing their fortunes because he would not *change his mind*. No, we must go to Gretna Green. It is the only way we will be together."

"No. I will not even consider it. You are far too important to me, and I could not bear to see you take the brunt of people's disdain. I will find a way. I just need you to be patient."

"There is no time. He is dragging me off to Bath within a few days!" Dinah realized she had raised her voice. This was not the time to appear emotional. If she was to persuade John to take a risk, she would need to sound logical, and demonstrate she was calm and understood the consequences of her proposal, or he would never agree and Dinah would be forced to part from him.

Her thoughts raced for an alternate solution. "Tell him I am ruined, that there is no choice, and we must wed immediately."

John looked at her, horrified. "What? I must approach your father and inform him that I bedded his daughter while living as a guest in his home? What purpose would that serve?"

"He would agree to a wedding."

"And your relationship with him, as well as mine, would be irreparably damaged. You love your father. Nay, I cannot be the cause of dissension between the two of you. He is your only family, and I know what it is to lose one's family. I could never be the reason for such a breach as the one I have suffered these past few years."

Dinah jumped to her feet, angry with him for his short-sighted views. "I think you care too much about what other people think and not enough about me—about us!"

"Dinah, I swear I will find a way. I will meet with my brother or with Halmesbury or ... anyone ... to discuss potential solutions. I will do right by you *and* ensure your reputation is maintained. Please, just give me a chance to make this right."

"If I am forced to leave for Bath, I shall never forgive you. *We* are more important than reputations or relationships. You must stand up to my father and demand we are wed forthwith."

John stood up to tower over her. "I will make this right, my heart. I swear it. Please, do not ask me to ruin the woman I love. Be patient."

"The woman you love is already ruined, you ... you ... lout!" Dinah could not take any more of this. She couldn't believe he would allow her father to stand in the way of their future—their destiny. He would allow her to be taken away from him on a ridiculous husband hunt for a man of consequence. She could not believe her father had rejected John's suit. Were all the men in her life imbeciles? She made for the door. Perhaps she would go yell at her father about making her choices for her as if she were a child and not a woman of three and twenty.

John gently grasped her by the arm. "Dinah, I will find a way. Have I not proved I will do what it takes to claim you? I will find a way!"

Dinah's eyes were filling with tears. She was embarrassed and hurt; she felt betrayed by John's willingness to let matters stand as they were.

"I don't believe you. You took four years to act, and only after I threw myself at you. I don't believe you ever felt strongly about me, that you love me as I love you. You lack courage, John. You would be a man of consequence if you acted more like a man and less like a slave of society's expectations."

Dinah knew her words were truly hurtful, but she was so frustrated. She had come so close to realizing her dreams, but yet again she was being asked to wait while … while … *men* decided her fate. If she had been born a man, her father would have taught her how to run his empire, but instead she was forced to wait around like an unwanted wallflower until the men in her life took action. She was sick of it. She had thrown herself at John, given him her maidenhood, yet still he asked her to wait. It was not to be borne!

Wrenching her arm from his hold, she stormed out of the room to find her bedchamber. She had things to say to her father, but first she would collect herself and then … then she would begin her ruthless assault.

* * *

JOHN STALKED out of the Honeyfield home, determined to take a walk and clear his thoughts. He had to find a solution, but to do so he would need to calm down.

"You are no one of consequence ..."

"You lack courage, John ..."

"You do not know your place, and you are a coward for refusing to do your duty to King and country ..."

"Cringing, sniveling coward ..."

"No son of mine ..."

Echoes of the past blended with the present, and John wondered if he truly was of no consequence, despite the duke's encouragement. He knew Dinah was hurt and confused, in addition to anxious over their scandalous night together, which she had expected to remain hidden by their betrothal, but ... his old family had rejected him and now the new family he had acquired were repeating the same sentiments while rejecting him, too. If he thought it had been a terrible time when he was disinherited, it was nothing compared to his current state of loss.

He truly had tried to do what was right, but it appeared he must be making all the wrong decisions because no matter what he did, he seemed to land in the same place: alone. He had to persuade Dinah he would do what was right—

John leapt back just in time as a carriage sped by over the patch of roadway he had inadvertently stepped into without looking. The only thing that could make this day worse was if he was killed on a busy London street to leave Dinah abandoned and alone. Then it would be a certainty that she was with child, with his current lack of luck. Looking around, he plotted a course to the nearest park and thrust his thoughts aside to pay attention.

He would find a way to make this right, but he would do so without being killed in the process.

* * *

DINAH OPENED the door and walked into her father's study. The old man might be obstinate, but he was about to find out that the trait ran in the family.

He looked up with a scowl. "What the damnation? Does no one knock anymore?"

"Knocking is for fathers who pay attention to their daughters."

"*Zooks!* This day keeps getting worse."

"What is the meaning of what you have done? John is a fine man, and he will be an important man as soon as he is allowed to pursue his craft."

"Dinah, I am doing what is best for you. You may not see it now, but one day you will see I made the right decision for your future. Please, can we let this be?"

"I don't think so. I love him and I will be with him, one way or another. I will convince him to elope, if I must."

Papa turned beet red as he jumped to his feet. Despite her dark mood she almost choked, holding back a laugh to see her short father turn into the mythical, angry Rumpelstiltskin from the German folktales she had read as part of her language lessons. The forest-green tailcoat straining over his round belly and the fawn-colored pantaloons only added to the imagery.

"Did you already propose that to him?"

"I did."

"And what did the boy say?"

"Boy? He is a man who is nearly thirty years of age."

"WHAT DID HE SAY?"

Dinah huffed as her father howled at her. She looked away and then reluctantly admitted the truth. "He would not dishonor me in that manner."

Her father released an enormous sigh, his round figure

slumping back in his leather chair, and he rubbed his face with his hand, clearly relieved at her answer as his color returned to normal.

"You must have a man worthy of you, Dinah. You are strong-willed and a force to be reckoned with. It will take a man of powerful character to balance out a marriage with you. I know what is best and you must trust me."

"John is strong! He walked away from a life of privilege to forge his own path. That took courage and backbone. I thought you were his friend. I thought you knew that about him."

"John is not the man for you. We will find the man for you. We will take this tour together, and we will find a fine, strong gentleman who will make you forget all about Petti-grew and this foolish attachment you have developed. I would never have invited him into my home if I thought it would lead to this."

Dinah took steps forward. "Papa, please, he is a good man. He is honest and hardworking. He stands up for himself, and he has gained a good living on the strengths of his talent. He would make a caring, steadfast partner. You must reconsider!"

"We leave for Bath on Tuesday."

"But—"

"We leave for Bath on Tuesday. If we do not find suitable men there, we shall leave for Birmingham, and if that does not work … well, we will move on until we find a suitable husband."

"You may drag me all over the kingdom, but I shall never accept another man. I have found my man, and if I have to wait you out, then so be it." Dinah knew her words had an impact. She had said them with utter, determined certainty. She did not care how many years rolled by; she would never accept another man. *You cannot even if you desired it; your lack of virtue makes that a certainty.*

Dinah squashed the doubtful thought. It did not matter. She would still have been resolute in her course even if she did not have a shameful secret to hide.

Her father's expression displayed worry when he next spoke. "Dinah … dear girl … can you please trust me? I am doing what is best for you."

"I know what is truly best for me. It is my life, after all."

Her father's plump face grew determined, stubborn even. "A good daughter would respect her father's wishes."

"A good father would ask for his daughter's opinion on matters that concerned her future."

"We have reached an impasse, then?"

She tilted her head in agreement. "We have."

"Now we wait it out and see who is the victor?"

"Indeed."

"So be it. You will discover why my rivals call me the most persistent merchant in the realm. It is not because I bow to others."

"And I have studied your *persistence* for many years, so we will find out which Honeyfield is more persistent. It will be a wintry day in hell before I do what you want."

Her father nodded his balding head. "So be it. We leave for Bath on Tuesday."

CHAPTER 6

*W*alking along Rotten Row, John admitted to himself that he had made a terrible mistake. One he did not know how to rectify, but he had to find a way. Anticipating his meeting with Mr. Honeyfield, he had allowed his passions to overtake him. He had robbed Dinah of her future, unless he could persuade Dinah's father to accept his suit.

What could he possibly do to change the mind of her obstinate parent? The older man was accustomed to negotiating. Had there been any room in their negotiation, any opening or hint of what would change Honeyfield's mind?

As John racked his thoughts, he recalled the man's remark that if the marquess was still involved, he might have reconsidered. He picked up his pace in frustrated fury as he suddenly realized what would convince the man to accept

John's suit. *Fuck*, he thought he had made his choice and set his path, but now it appeared he would revisit his decision out of necessity. If he returned to the Pettigrew home, he could set this right, do right by Dinah, but what a choice it would force him to make.

The universe was proving to be a merciless wench, forcing him to choose between the work he loved and the woman he loved. Since he had dishonored Dinah, there was no contest between the two. He must repair the consequences from his unbridled passions, or he was not a gentleman. He must visit his father, grovel and beg for forgiveness, then don the soldier's uniform so he may rejoin the Pettigrew family. It would delegate writing to the role of hobby, something done in whatever spare time he could mete out of his day between obligations to the army and obligations to his new family.

As John thought of all his unwritten words, the ideas still in waiting for the day he wrote them, he felt a keen sense of loss. He would have to give up his works, as well as his newly acquired patronage with Halmesbury. His daring the past few days had been for naught because he had anticipated success prematurely and boxed himself in to the inevitable path laid out for him at birth. It appeared he would continue the Pettigrew family traditions through military service to their kingdom.

He could do it.

He would do it … for Dinah.

She deserved to be treated with honor and fortitude.

Decision made, John's feet came to a stop. He took a deep breath—a moment to experience the keen losses the day had brought, to breathe his last freedom before he ventured—hopefully—into the army after his father accepted his apology. As he breathed in, he noticed for the first time the aroma of green grass, of trees and flowers in bloom. Apparently, his Hessians had brought him to Hyde Park to pause at the side of the Serpentine River. Children played at the water's edge while vigilant nannies watched on. Couples walked by in fine clothing and sweet smiles, and the world continued on in total ignorance of John's struggles. His world was ending, but it affected no one but him. He drew another deep breath.

For Dinah, it would be worthwhile. For Dinah, he would do anything; anything to keep her safe from scandal and banishment from society. And, for Dinah, he would find a way for this new path to make sense, to work, so his wonderful beauty would be happy in the life he would build for her and their future family.

While he accepted his alternative course in life, John admitted that whether he had debauched his fair Dinah the night before or not, he would still have faced this awful choice between his work and his beloved this morning after his meeting with Mr. Honeyfield. Would it have made a difference to his decision if he was not required to do the honorable thing?

John thought of a future in which he pursued his career, but left Dinah behind. It was chilling to consider. He may have been an idiot for the past four years for not making his move, but for all intents and purposes, they had been in a devoted relationship for some time, whether voiced or not. There were no circumstances in which he could be happy without her at his side. Any words he wrote without her would be of loss and misery and, Lord knew, the world did not need yet another melancholy poet to spread words of tragedy.

Nay, no matter the events of the night before, he would still have chosen Dinah this morning. He would choose Dinah any morning. Every morning. Only an imbecile could walk away from such a perfect union of the souls expecting to experience that depth of connection again.

Concluding he would have always found himself at this moment, making this tough choice, somehow settled his mind, and his resentment melted away to leave the disappointment of lost dreams in its place. At least he would have Dinah to ease the transition back to his old life. Together they would make it work, build a good life. His muse would not allow him to dwell on the past or what could have been. They would make their happiness.

His Hessians turned for home, and he accepted his fate. No one would accuse Lord John Pettigrew any longer of being a man of no consequence once he donned his officer's uniform as the younger son of a marquess. Why did the world have to be so shallow that a man's worth was measured by his obedience to his illustrious family rather than by his own actions? The expectations of society were a noose around the neck of any freethinking man.

* * *

By the time he reached the Honeyfield home, John was exhausted from hours of walking. It was with some relief that he handed his overcoat to the footman, along with his favored beaver from his older brother. The reserved young man took the items before speaking. "Milord, you have a visitor waiting for you in the library."

"Visitor?"

"Yes, milord, he has been here for almost two hours." The footman bowed and walked away quickly. John suddenly realized that the young man had failed to say who the visitor was, but as John called out the question, he saw the servant had already vanished down the hall.

Damn! I need a damn drink, not a damn visitor! He had had

the worst two days, so dealing with a mystery visitor he was not expecting was the last thing he wanted to do. What he wanted to do was to find a very large tumbler of fine French brandy, an empty room, and mourn the career he was about to prematurely cancel to do right by the woman he loved. He needed to mourn before he had to visit the marquess's home in the morning to throw himself on his father's mercy. A man should be able to grieve the loss of his hopes and dreams in peace to collapse into a heap of soused exhaustion.

Stalking down the hall to the library, John resolved to greet his visitor, give him a few moments of his time, and then unceremoniously show the man out. Within half an hour, he could be in his bedchamber with a decanter of brandy to keep him company. It was his last night as his own man, as a man who shaped his own destiny, and it should be celebrated.

He entered the room and came to a halt, looking about for his visitor.

After a moment, he observed that at the far end of the library, framed by the windows, was a tall, slender man dressed in a rich, dark gray tailcoat and dove gray trousers in the fashion of Beau Brummel. The figure had his back to the door, his posture was ramrod, and his hair was thick, almost white. John scowled in confusion at the interruption. Who could this be? It was at that moment in which he noticed that his enigmatic visitor had his hands clasped behind his back while he viewed the gardens beyond the glass, which caused butterflies to take flight in the region of John's stomach. There was something familiar about the pose ... had he somehow conjured—

"Father?"

His visitor stiffened, then slowly turned. Regal in his dove-gray vest, snow-white shirt, and crisp white cravat, the figure revealed himself. It was, as suspected, the marquess.

Mayhap John's troubled musings had summoned his parent into the Honeyfield home because the very man John was to seek out the following day now stood before him. It could not be comprehended; they had not spoken in the years since his father had demanded he pack his things and depart the family home.

"Son, I have been waiting for you."

Instantly on the defense, John retorted, "I can't be blamed for that, I did not know to expect you!" Realizing it was not the best opening for his intention to apologize and beg for the old man's mercy, John bit back his emotions silently as he sought how to retract his thoughtless outburst.

"I apologize, John. I did not mean to sound critical. I was merely stating an observation, but it was a poor beginning after so many years apart."

John's jaw dropped in astonishment. The marquess was apologizing? To him? "I—"

"No, wait. I have something to say, and I want to get it out. I have mulled over how to have this conversation for hours, and I think it best if I say what I came to say before-before—I think it best I say what I came to say ..." His father trailed off, his bright hazel eyes appearing ... diffident?

John was dumbstruck. He had never seen the marquess unsure of himself, but his austere, all-knowing parent seemed to struggle for words. Realizing his father was looking at him as if waiting for a cue, John gave a quick nod of agreement.

"I had a most awkward meeting late yesterday with the Duke of Halmesbury. He made an appointment to see me, about what I did not know. But he is a very important man, so I did not refuse his request and we met. I thought perhaps he wanted to discuss a bill he plans to put forward at Westminster. But to my great surprise, the meeting was about you."

The marquess hesitated and looked away. He appeared to be composing himself, and John's thoughts ran riotously as he tried to anticipate where this conversation was leading. Halmesbury had been pressed for time when John had met with him yesterday, mentioning he had an important appointment. Could it be the duke had been referring to a meeting with his own father?

"The duke brought your published works with him ..." The marquess trailed off once more. "During our discussion, I came to the uncomfortable realization that I have been in the wrong. That I had wronged you by my failure to communicate with you, to compromise. To make an effort to understand you."

The marquess looked thoughtful as he studied the toes of his polished black shoes. "We are so different, you and I, are we not, John?"

John nodded his agreement. They were oil and water in their opinions and interests, but he had never thought to hear the marquess acknowledge his son had a right to his own views.

"I truly believed you were a coward to refuse the commission, but Halmesbury explained the situation to me in a new light. In his opinion, it took true courage for you to walk away, to stick to your convictions. He read me some of your words, and they were astonishing. I had no idea you ... He said talent and commitment deserved praise, not disinheritance, which is why he has agreed to become your patron. I am mortified to be corrected by such an important man ..." The marquess looked exceedingly embarrassed at his admission, suddenly finishing his thoughts in a quick burst of words. "Like an infant who threw his peas, but the duke is right and *I* should have been your patron these many years, not him. Can you ... can you forgive me?"

John stared at his father, his mouth agape, not speaking

for several moments as he tried to make sense of this pronouncement. He could not believe the duke had taken the time to intervene on his behalf, to approach the marquess to speak with him on the matter. Halmesbury had always been a peacemaker, but this was … was … so much trouble to go to for a friend he had not seen in years. Unbelievably, it had worked! John could not believe his father was standing before him. And an apology? It was incomprehensible. The marquess was pure aristocratic arrogance and never considered himself at fault. In all the years living in his father's home, John had never heard him apologize to anyone for anything.

As the moments ticked, the marquess's stern face displayed unease. "Son, I am offering to provide you with your own estate that will produce a healthy income. I would offer to reinstate your allowance, but the duke pointed out that given our history, and the fact I disinherited you, an allowance would not inspire the confidence and security you would need to focus on your writing. As a landowner, you will never be beholden to anyone again. My man of business is looking through my estates as we speak to recommend which one would be comparable to the allowance I have withheld. Or I will purchase an estate if there is no suitable one among my holdings. Will you forgive me? I have missed you, and I want you back in my—our—lives."

John shook his head in confusion before striding forward to grasp the older man. "Father … I … How … There are no words …" He embraced the marquess. His father froze, surprised, not quite returning the embrace but allowing it. After a few moments, John stepped back.

"I would say prideful words … such as, I have made my way without you. I don't need your money, or something equally foolhardy and stubborn, but I am so happy to see you. And your timing … There are no words to express how important your timing is. My own estate? That would indeed be an incredible gift. Should I accept it?" he wondered out loud. "Does it make me less of a man in my own right?"

The marquess looked ashamed as he stared down at the gold signet ring on his finger. "It is your birthright, son. I should not have taken it away or accused you of being an immature boy. But you were always so headstrong, and I thought I was in the right—that the military would turn you into a man. I did not recognize that you were already a man who was standing up for himself. That I was demanding that you be the man *I* envisioned without acknowledging your right to forge your own path. Those words the duke recited from your volume ... you were born for this, and I should never have stood in your way. I am so proud of what you have achieved on your own, and now ... now I would like to contribute to your future as I should have done all along. Long after we have turned to dust, your words will remain in the world as the legacy of our generation of Pettigrews. I would be proud to assist you."

John thrust a clenched fist to his mouth, overcome with emotion. He had been so sure he would have to choose between his career and the woman he loved, but at the final hour, his friend had interceded and taken measures to secure his future. He wished he knew how to repay the duke for displaying such favor toward him.

Swallowing hard, he asked the question burning in his mind. "Am I permitted to come to Sunday family dinners?"

The marquess huffed a laugh. "We will resurrect family dinners so that you may attend. Your mother and your brother have been steadfast in expressing their disagreement over how I handled the situation with you, so there have not been family dinners in some time. If the duke had not interceded, however, I would have soon sought you out myself so I could restore household equilibrium. You have been much in my thoughts of late, and the duke's visit was opportune, for I needed a … a kick to be spurred into action. It is good to see you again, son. I should not have been such a self-righteous fool, nor been so quick to discard my own blood."

John huffed a happy sigh as he walked over to the drinks cabinet and poured out two modest drams. Bringing the tumblers over, he handed one to his father. With a voice roughened by emotion, he made his second proposal to an important peer in as many days. "As we are both adult men now, Father, let us share a drink and raise a toast to the Pettigrews, shall we?"

CHAPTER 7

Noble gestures, overtures to be wrought;
the future with unknowns do be fraught.

inah reached the bottom step and looked around the hall, wondering if John would join them for services this one last time before she and her father departed for Bath. Her heart was a leaden weight in her chest. She had not seen John since their argument, since the morning she had begged him to run away with her to Gretna Green and he had refused her.

She knew he had promised to find a way to change her father's mind, but deep down she knew it would take a miracle. Despite his recent actions and good fortune, she could not see any likely outcome other than embarking to Bath with her sole parent, leaving her sweet John behind.

Not that her father was a cruel man, he simply had—in his mind—made a sound business decision and, as such, and being famously obstinate about his work, he would not consider a love match more important than protecting his business empire from erosion. If John was still connected to the marquess … but then if John and his father were on speaking terms, she would never have met the confounded gentleman who had stolen her heart.

Peter Honeyfield had been born with no wealth or connections, the son of a poor cobbler, and had fought tooth and nail for every success he had ever achieved, so Dinah understood why her father was so adamant, but not why he could not see John's potential. Each time she had argued with him, she had exhausted each of them further, but neither would shift their position even an inch. She knew the most compelling argument would have been John's noble lineage, but without the support of his family and their connections, *that* argument was rendered moot. She would be forced to give up her love for the sake of textiles, factories, and account balances while much less fortunate women had the opportunity to choose their own husbands.

Dinah had experienced a range of emotions over the past day, from anger to grief. Currently, she felt … numb. She had exhausted her ideas; she had exhausted herself with tears, and she had exhausted her father with pleading to reconsider his decision. But Papa was adamant she would get over it and that what mattered was the right man with the right skills and connections to take care of her and her inheritance once he was gone. He stated each time that security was more important than any frivolous emotions and she would come to realize that he was correct in his assertions once she had experienced more of life.

While Dinah stood lost in her thoughts, tying the moss-green ribbons of the bonnet that the footman had just handed her, she failed to notice that her father and John had entered the hall and were shrugging into their respective overcoats. Her spirits lifted to see her dear poet, but she was unable to talk to him with her father standing sternly by. She wondered if he had uncovered any solutions as he had promised, but as her eyes searched his face, she found only a grim resolution. No fortunate turn of events, then. This might be one of the last times she would see him, and they could not even hug or talk openly.

Fighting back tears, she greeted the men who murmured their replies. The footman opened the front door, and in a group, they descended the front steps. John held out a gloved hand to assist her into the carriage, quickening Dinah's pulse as she clasped his hand for a fraction longer than necessary. Those strong, slim hands had been on her naked skin less than forty-eight hours earlier, bringing her to passionate release, but she would likely never feel his touch again.

Aching with suppressed grief, she moved into the far corner to stare blindly out the window as the two men embarked and took their seats. She fancied the air was thick with tension, but she did not spare a glance at either man to confirm her perception. They were both a great disappointment to her, and what was there to say that had not already been said?

The carriage lurched forward, and they were on their way to St. James's Church, which her father favored. Dinah personally preferred the smaller church they had attended before moving to Mayfair, but with their new home, Papa had insisted they attend the fashionable church to rub shoulders with elite members of society. Dinah herself had little time for his so-called noteworthy people, preferring her friends to be easy to converse with rather than gossiping old wives, debutantes, and dandies overdressed to impress other gossiping old wives, debutantes, and overdressed dandies. What was the point? She would gladly live on John's annual income and forgo the latest gowns and bonnets in order to be married to the man she loved. Instead, she was expected to place great value on these people and what they thought of her. *Zounds!* She did not even like spending time with them.

Their carriage came to a halt, but she did not prepare to dismount; now they would wait in a lengthy line of private carriages for other fashionable elite to disembark in front of the church. It was interminable, so she remained with her eyes fixed on passersby, lost in her thoughts about what it would be like to leave John behind and know that when she finally returned to London, he would no longer reside in the Honeyfield home. He would have moved on while she fought with her father to remain unmarried. Even if, eventually, she had wanted to marry an agreeable suitor, she could not, as her lack of virtue would be revealed.

Damn, John! How could he consider that eloping to Gretna Green would dishonor her, instead forcing her to meet young gentlemen the width and breadth of England while she hid her scandalous depravity? She threw an angry glance at him, sitting calmly and composed in the opposite corner of the seat. Had he no shame?

She dully sank back into depression as she admitted she would have chosen spinsterhood regardless of their one night of passion. No other man could compare with her true love; if she could not be with him, then no other man would do.

* * *

PRESENTLY THEY MADE their way into the customary pew near the middle of the church, and Dinah straightened her skirts to take a seat on the hardwood bench. The large church was buzzing with talk while people piled into it, but all that Dinah could think of was what a sweet sorrow it was to feel John's trousered leg press gently against hers when he took his seat. She stared down at his polished black Hessians and thought about how they had been strewn across the floor of his room two nights earlier when she and John had slaked their passions in each other's arms. How he had lovingly run his hand over her thighs and composed sweet sonnets to her beauty after they had made love. How she might never lie in his arms again, and that some other maiden would one day be his wife while she was forced to avoid a union because of her secret shame.

Her eyes prickled with threatening tears, and she turned her head to stare sightlessly up at the stained-glass windows while people continued to take their seats. She did not know how much time had passed when she noticed the vicar had arrived and was shuffling through his notes. Her thoughts wandered once more to contemplate nothing in particular, but skipped between past encounters with John and future assemblies she would attend in far-flung cities.

She felt John nudge her leg with his own, which brought her out of her reverie to look up at his face, her brow arched in question. He indicated the vicar with a curt lifting of his chin, and she scowled in confusion but looked to the vicar to see what John was pointing out.

"William Jones and Jane McQuire. Thomas Davies and Mary Tunnell," the vicar intoned.

Dinah turned back to scowl at John. What did she care about the reading of the banns? He smiled down at her, then indicated again that she pay attention to the vicar.

"James Upton and Elizabeth Savage."

She continued to glare at him. What did her infernal almost-intended want with her? Her heart was breaking, and now he was correcting her for woolgathering during services.

"John Fitzgerald Pettigrew and Dinah Honeyfield."

She had not the patience to listen to the vicar drone on about other happy couples—*Wait, what did the vicar just say?* She spun her head forward to stare at the vicar, but he, predictably, did not repeat himself and continued on as he did every Sunday.

She turned back to stare with wide eyes at John. "Did he …" she mumbled below her breath. To her wonderment, John stared into her eyes and then gave a nod. "What … How …?"

He leaned down to whisper in her ear. "It's not formal. We offered the vicar a healthy donation to slip our names in at the end, but we did not give seven days' notice so we will obtain a Common License. But you deserve a public declaration that cannot be revoked after all you have endured the past few days."

Dinah spun her head to the left to find her father repressing a smile; his nostrils, lips, and even his ginger whiskers were quivering with the effort as he resolutely stared up to the altar. *It is true? Papa has consented to our marriage?* Suddenly the room brightened into a vivid display of color and sound as her spirits soared.

John had done it! She did not know what he had done, but he had done something to persuade her father. She lifted her gloved hand to cover her mouth in awe, gasping back the sob of joy threatening to escape her lips, then exhaled a deep sigh as she found herself giddy with relief.

John surreptitiously grabbed her other hand from her lap, brought it to rest between their thighs, hidden in the folds of her gown, and clasped it within his own. He squeezed gently, as if asking her a question, to which she squeezed back in heady acceptance as tears of happiness quietly streaked down her cheeks. Her almost-betrothed, *nay*, her *actual* betrothed discreetly handed her his handkerchief.

* * *

LATER THAT DAY, she found John in the library, drinking a celebratory coffee with her father. She joined them while a maid followed her in with a tea tray. Leaning forward to pour her tea, Dinah settled back with her cup and saucer.

Her father cleared his throat and stood. "I trust the two of you have much to discuss, and I am expecting a visitor shortly, so I will leave you to it." With that, he straightened the sleeves of his tailcoat and left the room.

Dinah turned to John with enormous eyes. "How did you do it?"

John's lean face broke into a joyous smile as he reached forward to grab her hand and lift it to his lips. "First, I will tell you how I did not do it. I was prepared to do it, but it became unnecessary. I was to approach my father, beg him to forgive me, and accept the commission he wanted for—"

"Oh, John, no!"

"I promised you I would make this right, so I would have done it. I would have done anything to spare you from ruin. Instead, the duke, with no warning of what he intended, made an appointment with my father and set him in his place about how he handled his family commitments. Halmesbury recited my poetry to the marquess, who was forced to listen to a superior, and then the duke insisted my father rectify the situation."

"He did not!"

"Indeed, he did. And Father had a change of heart. So just as I had concluded that the only path forward was to relinquish my career and return to my father's household for the appropriate connections to persuade your father I was earnest, the marquess appeared here—in this library—for a visit and asked me to forgive him. I was ... speechless."

"And that was sufficient to change my father's mind about our union?"

"No, my love. As part of reconciling, my father promised

me an estate of my own with a regular, healthy income so I may be independent, and he reinstated the family connections. That was what I approached your father with, and this time your father agreed I would make a suitable husband." John smiled, his eyes narrowing. "I suspect Mr. Honeyfield may have been playing a long game with us, though, forcing my hand so I would take action to restore the connection. He did not seem surprised when I approached him the second time and was very amenable, not to mention the numerous hints he had dropped at our first meeting regarding my connection to the marquess. Your father is an astute businessman."

Dinah thought about the events of the past two days, reaching the conclusion John was right. It was just the type of maneuver her father was infamous for. He had wanted John to marry her all along, but he wanted her to marry into a powerful family in the bargain. Her father was a deliberate businessman who had seen an opportunity to ascend the social ladder through her relationship and manipulated events to achieve his purpose. She should have deduced what he was up to, because Papa himself was still committed to her late mother many years after her passing and had never sought a new wife to take her place. Emotion was not an important factor, indeed! Her father had tricked her and John, too, it would seem.

"That-that ... why, that ... *damnit!* The old goat did do it on purpose! Why would he do this to me? To my state of mind?"

John huffed, understanding dawning across his face. Dinah could not think what clarity he was experiencing because she was still confused. "I believe your father saw the same potential in me that you saw. However, in his case, he desired that I *prove* my worth. Honestly, I cannot state with any confidence that I would have agreed to reunite with the marquess without your father's decisive refusal to provide me with incentive, even with the duke's intercession. I may have turned my father away out of wounded pride. The situation with you made the reconciliation imperative, so I cannot fault your father's contrivance. Even the planned trip to Bath provided an additional incentive to act quickly. Do you think he intended it to do so?"

"Of course!" Dinah groaned, shaking her head in disbelief. "How did we not suspect this? No one goes to Bath in the summer! Papa must have counted on it spurring me into action, thus spurring you into action. It certainly did that, after years of allowing our relationship to stagnate with no motion forward or backward. He never intended to leave London, that devil!"

John threw his back against the seat to stare thoughtfully at the ceiling. "Good Lord, you are correct. The season in Bath is over, and it is likely empty at this time of the year. What an elaborate ruse he has pulled, closing up portions of the house as if he truly intended on departing."

"He has made me a fool," Dinah lamented, smarting that her father had foxed her into throwing herself into John's arms.

John lifted himself from the settee and dropped onto one knee as he grasped her hand and lifted it to his tanned cheek. "I, for one, am very glad I was forced into action. This week has been … indescribable. Invigorating. And now I can claim you as my bride. I did not have the confidence to take the steps I needed to take, but his invented trip to Bath was precisely the incitement I needed to spring into action."

He fervently kissed her hand. "I apologize for the whirlwind of emotions you endured while I worked out how to be worthy of you, and I am grateful you pushed me into action. I love you, my heart. I can't wait to make you my wife, in truth."

Dinah stared into his hazel eyes, flecked with fascinating depths of gray, green, and brown, and her heart beat with so much joy she was sure it would break out of her chest. The future she had envisioned the night she and John had first met was finally coming about, and her destiny was at hand. Impulsively, she leaned forward and pressed a kiss to his firm lips.

This time, it gratified her that it was not clumsy and ill-timed, but rather precise and well-executed. She was belatedly becoming good at this kissing.

Oh, sweet thoughts of blood and bonds.

"Pettigrew! You have arrived, dear chap! Come in, come in." A jovial duke stood on the steps to his honey-colored country home, Avonmead, and beckoned John and his wife forward. "I am so happy to see you. You are the last to arrive for our little Christmas house party."

John and Dinah ascended the stone steps and entered the hall behind Halmesbury. They swiveled their heads up in awe to stare at the exquisite frescos painted on the lofty hall ceiling.

"My lady, Clinton will show you to your rooms, and my bride will meet you for tea once you have had a chance to freshen up. Take as long as you like. Could I steal your husband for a few moments to have a drink?" Dinah looked at John, who tilted his head in agreement.

"I believe taking a rest would be a good idea, my love."

She nodded, her gray eyes clouded with weary reverence as she was shown up the majestic staircase of the ducal home. The banisters were bedecked with fresh, green

Christmas boughs, and the hall smelled like a veritable forest of firs had been cut down for the merry decorations. John watched his wife's petite frame swaying up the stairs. It gladdened him that she would have an opportunity to rest; the journey from London had been long and the roads rough. Traveling in her condition had taken its toll, and he had only accepted the duke's invitation because she was only a few weeks along and excited to meet the duke and his bride. Nevertheless, they had made several stops on their journey from London to Wiltshire due to the nausea she was struggling with.

John turned back to the duke and shook his head in confusion. "A drink? It's only ten in the morning, Halmesbury?"

The duke laughed jubilantly. John blinked in consternation. The change in the usually reclusive duke was astounding; he was positively floating on air. Was Halmesbury's change in mood something to do with the new duchess he had recently wed?

"I meant coffee, dear friend. Just coffee. Do you recall the last time we shared coffee?"

John thought back to earlier in the year when he had encountered the duke outside of Hatchards bookshop. Their lives had been altered since that day many months ago. For one, they both were newly married, and John was reconciled with his family, whom they would visit directly after Halmesbury's holiday house party.

"Come, Pettigrew, let us go to my study for that coffee, and I can enlighten you on how your article in *The Gentleman's Magazine* has affected not only my own life, but that of another old friend, too."

John followed Halmesbury down the hall and into an elegant study, where he saw a tray of coffee laid out. By the window stood a man with rigid military bearing, his rich green tailcoat well-suited to his copper-colored hair, staring out into the park.

"Lewis, my guest has arrived. This is Jacob Lewis, Pettigrew." Turning to the man at the window, the duke explained, "This is John Pettigrew, the one who wrote the article on me."

The gentleman at the window turned and stared at him. "Lord John Pettigrew?"

John nodded.

"Good Lord, man." The man stormed across the room and, before John could react, threw his arms around him in a bearlike embrace, almost lifting him off his feet in his enthusiasm.

John stared over at Halmesbury with a questioning look as he patted the man's shoulder awkwardly.

Halmesbury smiled benignly in response, apparently not in the least surprised by his friend's strange behavior. "I have looked forward to your arrival. You see, old chap, you not only brought my bride to my doorstep with your article, but my friend experienced his own happy outcome after he eventually acquired his copy of the August edition of *The Gentleman's Magazine*. But that is his story to tell if he wishes to do so. Let us partake in some bitter black beverage so you may hear how your writing brought us both joy this year."

The gentleman let John go and stepped back. He thought he saw a sheen in the man's brilliant turquoise eyes when he turned to make his way over to the aromatic coffee steaming on the tray. John wondered how his article could have brought tears to the eyes of, he guessed, a former soldier as he followed the duke's odd friend to take a seat on the red and ivory striped Chesterfield sofa, which turned out to be quite comfortable despite its grand appearance.

Halmesbury dropped his tall frame into an intricately carved wooden chair across from them. "Pettigrew is the soul of discretion, Lewis, if you would like to share your story. He won't breathe a word of it to anyone except, mayhap, to his vivacious wife. Fiery locks of sunset exactly as described, Pettigrew."

Jacob Lewis tipped his head in acknowledgment. "Where do I begin?"

"At the beginning, old chap. Tell John about how you read his article." The duke was ebullient in his response, and John found himself most intrigued as he leaned forward to hear the stranger's tale.

AUTHOR'S NOTE

Recently, I experienced a moment of enlightenment about how reading had shaped my life. As a reader, one develops an ability to think from other viewpoints, to consider multiple ideas, and to visit many more places than one could travel in one lifetime.

Reading helped me understand the troubles of the people I worked with in drug rehabilitation; not just the addict, but their family members and their concerns, too. I could empathize with the people I worked with no matter their backgrounds, culture, or belief systems because of the thousands of books I had consumed that helped me to place myself in the shoes of another, and thus understand them despite our differences.

Later, being well-read, I could coach different flavors of people on how to sell more effectively within the boundaries of their personalities, and their strengths and weaknesses, in order to connect effectively with a wider range of people than they could have without coaching.

Without the books I have read, I would be a very different and much less-enlightened person.

Some of the many books I read were non-fiction, but a vast majority were fiction. I saw, for the first time, the role stories have played in forming my understanding of the world, which led me to embrace my own passion to tell stories. Something I realized I had been doing all along to illustrate points of view within every field I had worked in. I finally put my stories to paper (or keyboard, to be more accurate).

This prequel was my homage to the great value of story-tellers within our culture. In the next stories learn how John Pettigrew's article in *The Gentleman's Magazine* impacted both Jacob Lewis in *The Captain's Wife* and Halmesbury himself in *The Duke Wins a Bride*. All three of these tales are my testament to the power of the written word and the great distances that ideas travel to change lives.

Turn the page to start reading The Captain's Wife.

NINA JARRETT

PREQUEL

CHAPTER 1

PRESENT DAY, OCTOBER 1818

"*L*ydia."

Her hand froze on the brass door handle. She would recognize that deep velvety voice anywhere. It made her heart leap with joy and her veins freeze in horror. Slowly, she turned around, praying her vivid imagination was playing tricks on her. Her eyes searched and found what she was afraid of: her husband, tall and painfully handsome, standing on the lowest step.

He looked different from the last time she had seen him. His shock of coppery hair stirred in the breeze, and his intense eyes, which changed hue from blue to green depending on his mood, were currently a deep shade of turquoise and fixed on her own. Her heart raced and her mouth went dry with apprehensive excitement while her eyes traveled over his freckled snub nose, wide cheekbones, firm mouth, and strong, triangular jaw. The rain clouds that threatened cast a strange light and framed him with deep grays, adding to the drama of their overdue reunion.

After three long years, Jacob, her husband, had found her.

* * *

THEY STARED at each other for several moments before he spoke again, his voice husky with emotion. "I don't know whether to shake you or kiss you, but unless you want one or the other to occur out here on the roadway, I suggest you let me come inside?"

Lydia jumped, remembering where she was as her eyes darted up and down the deserted street. "Of course," she murmured as she turned to open the red door, then led the way through the dark hall and into the front room. Jacob followed her, and while Lydia hurried to light the oil lamps, she was aware that he took in the sparse furnishings, his eyes settling on her father's large leather-bound Bible laid out on the escritoire by the front window.

Finishing her task, she looked up, embarrassed that her hands were trembling with repressed emotion, to find Jacob standing near the stone fireplace and gazing at her. She noted with surprise that he was wearing a burgundy tailcoat with brass buttons, reminiscent of his customary scarlet uniform coatee. Instead of his uniform whites, he wore a fawn waistcoat and pantaloons. A white linen cravat was tied around his neck in place of a military black stock, and rather than his black soldier riding boots, he wore polished brown Hessians. A gray beaver was in his hand, no evidence of his black soldier cap, and his hair had grown out to a mess of curly locks that her fingers itched to comb and smooth back from his face. He was the very picture of the perfect country gentleman paying a call on the home of an acquaintance.

"Lydia Lewis, as I live and breathe. Or am I to call you Mrs. Thorne?"

"You are no longer in the army?" she blurted.

"That is correct. I sold my captain's commission nearly

three years ago—when I returned from war and learned you were missing."

Lydia bobbed her head in distracted acknowledgment. "How did you find me?"

Jacob took the magazine rolled up under his arm, shaking it out so she could see the title. "*The Gentleman's Magazine* ran an interesting article recently." Jacob opened the magazine and found what he was looking for. " 'His Grace, the Duke of Halmesbury, renowned for his estimable charitable work, recently oversaw the renovations and restaffing of The Halmesbury Home for Children' … et cetera, et cetera … 'appointing his own esteemed housekeeper, Mrs. Lydia Thorne, as the director of the home.' "

"You remembered?"

Jacob scowled, tossing his head in affront, which set his coppery waves bouncing as if they had a life of their own. "I remember everything … I remember that we played make-believe as children by the river and your title was Princess Lydia of Thorne. I remember we read each other poetry and novels in the meadows when I came home for breaks from Eton. I remember how you looked, what you wore at our anvil wedding when that blacksmith presided over our hurried vows in Gretna Green. I vividly recollect the letters you sent me when I was shipped out to war with the French madman. How I prayed to survive my wounds, so as to not abandon you, as I lost consciousness on the blood-soaked grounds of Waterloo. My memory of fighting a fever in a field hospital for weeks, while awaiting word … any word … from my wife is etched indelibly on my mind. I also can't help but recollect the exact moment when I returned home and was told of your midnight disappearance at the end of June 1815. So, yes, I recognized your alias and, after years of searching, I finally worked out where to find you."

Lydia stared at him with rounded eyes, her chest

constricted in horror at the thought of Jacob injured. Until today she had not been certain he had survived the Hundred Days after Napoleon's infamous escape from Elba. To see him in the flesh, to confirm that he indeed lived, filled her head with a riot of emotions—predominantly light-headed relief that he was alive, well, and with no visible evidence of permanent injury marring his physique.

Jacob grimaced as he looked away. "Unfortunately … the one thing I did not remember was telling you fourteen years ago about how I had attended school with Halmesbury, and that he was a kind and honorable man—a true gentleman. I only recently recalled, while reading this article, that I had stated that if I was ever in need, he was the one person other than you whom I would trust with my life. That, and, of course, that he owed me a favor for tutoring him when he had difficulty with his Latin lessons, and that he was eager to repay the favor. If I had, in fact, remembered our conversation in your father's rose garden, I would have found you long before today."

Lydia dropped her gaze to stare sightlessly at her entwined fingers, unsure what to say. Her day of reckoning had arrived.

CHAPTER 2

Captain Jacob Lewis listened to the carriage wheels striking the bumpy road and found it difficult to comprehend that he was finally home on a much sought-after leave. The past few months had been hellish, and he was not certain that the diversions of a peacetime army officer were suited to him. Drinking and staying out all hours as he had been were leaving a stain on his soul. Whereas his fellow officers were more than happy to take advantage of the light-skirts who accompanied any respectable army garrison, he had thought himself above such lowly pursuits. Until he had made the mistake of engaging in a torrid affair with an officer's wife. He shook his head at his arrogance, at how he had thought that his lascivious activities were superior to paying a woman coin for her favors.

It had all unraveled many weeks ago when the same officer had returned to the barracks, in his cups, and lamented his broken heart, certain that his beloved wife was having an affair. It was in that moment that Jacob had recognized himself as a cad. Rather than being superior to his skirt-chasing fellow soldiers, he had become despicable scum that had betrayed a loyal friend—someone whom he might rely on in battle one day.

This rude awakening had caused Jacob to re-examine his life. He had spent years avoiding commitment, treating girls in a glib manner with the weak excuse that his parents' marriage had been disastrous and his mother faithless. All the while, he had continued his correspondence with his childhood friend, Lydia, the vicar's daughter from his village. Sweet Lydia, with her dainty form, sable brown locks, chocolate eyes, and a straight nose that crinkled when she teased him. As thoughts of Lydia had filled his head, he had become obsessed with returning to his innocence and honor with her light presence to guide him. He could no longer deny that the girl of his dreams had been at his side all of these years. Her quick mind had challenged him to learn, in order to out-argue her in their debates. Her love of books had enticed him to discover a world beyond their village in the north of England, helping him excel at Eton. Her love of rambles and exploring the meadows and glades had caused his dedication to exercise that had shaped his form into the hard body of a soldier. She had been his best friend as long as he could remember, but it was only recently that he had admitted what an enticing, incomparable woman she had become.

While his conscience had struggled over his recent poor behavior, letters from Lydia had been the highlights of his weeks, lifting his spirits and reminding him that he had once been honorable and, if he worked hard, he could be again. But even as his spirits had been lifted, his baser impulses had led him to enjoy erotic, sweaty dreams of claiming her sweet, rose-colored lips. Of gazing into her chocolate brown eyes while she writhed beneath him, and of taking her when she opened her thighs to receive him. Their inevitable union had been written in the stars—a union he had been avoiding since he was a lad of sixteen and he had first noticed she was a desirable woman. Now it was the only thing that made sense in the mad, idle peacetime world he lived in.

He was almost certain she wanted him. She had never encouraged any other courtship, as if she had been waiting for him to notice her. He recalled her shy glances over the past few years that he had ignored while he sowed his oats. But never at home, never where Lydia would be forced to witness it. He acknowledged with shame that he had been saving her for when he was ready. Ready to be responsible and behave like a man. In the interim, his conduct had become ugly as he enjoyed himself at the expense of others.

He was no longer willing to be glib and irresponsible, so he had secured this leave to return home and declare his intentions. A formal courtship would begin, and perhaps on his next leave he could wed her. He only hoped he had not waited too long to claim his long-desired destiny with Lydia—it had been several months since he had seen her last, but she had not noted any courtships in her correspondence. Nevertheless, his nerves rattled him as the carriage drew closer to the vicarage. Lydia was five-and-twenty, having lost too many years waiting for him to come to his senses. He hoped she was still waiting for him, since God knew he did not deserve her. He would do anything to gain her hand and recover the lightness of spirit he found in her company. There was not a soul anywhere who made him feel alive or challenged him as she did, and there would be no replacing her if she had moved on to someone more deserving—less selfish—than he had proved to be.

* * *

JACOB KNOCKED on the vicarage door and waited out in the chill for a response. He heard sounds from within and drew a deep breath when the door opened and he beheld his Lydia's beloved face. And his heart froze.

Lydia's chocolate eyes were red and swollen; she was dressed in black, and her fair, creamy skin was dulled with grief.

"What has happened?"

She looked up at him, her eyes welling with unshed tears. "Papa has passed away. He had an apoplexy a few days ago. The vicar from the next town held a service for him this morning."

Jacob was shocked. The vicar had been a robust man in his late forties, seemingly invincible. "I am so sorry, sweet princess. Please, let me come inside and comfort you."

With a nod, she turned to walk down the low corridor. Jacob swung the door shut and followed her into the cozy sitting room. A fire burned in the hearth, and everywhere he looked, books had been taken from shelves and stacked on available surfaces. Gingerly, he removed a pile and placed it on the floor so he might take a seat close to his grieving friend.

As he took in her drooping shoulders, his heart sank. So much for his plans to declare his intentions to court her; there could not be a more inappropriate time. His love would have to wait.

"What is the reason for all the scattered books?"

"Papa has left me a little money but not enough to live on indefinitely. I will have to move out as soon as a new vicar is appointed, so I need to sell Papa's books and begin searching for a position. I think I would make a fine governess, don't you?" She gave a wan smile. "At least I could work with children, because it appears I have settled into permanent spinsterhood."

Jacob felt the blood draining from his face and fingers while he attempted to control his breathing. If Lydia took a position as a governess, he may never see her again. This is what death must be like, with one's life flashing before one's eyes, except instead of the life he had led, he saw the years he would have had with Lydia. Their wedding vows, their first home, her swollen with child, and their babe learning to walk. All of these dreams vanishing before him as a twist of fate drove them apart. Swallowing hard, he managed to say, "I'm so sorry, Lydia. I wish I could have been here for you a week ago."

She looked up into his eyes and smiled. "Dear Jacob, it is enough to see you now. I am so glad I have an opportunity to see you one last time before I leave the village." She drew back to give him an appraising glance. "So fine in your captain's uniform, I am so glad Sir James was able to secure the commission for you!"

Jacob's heart tightened. His dear girl was in mourning and still found the presence of mind to note his recent ascension in rank. This might not be the right time to declare his love and begin a courtship, but he could not let her disappear from his life as if she had never existed, a distant echo of a beautiful dream he had once had.

He must do something. Jumping out of his chair, he paced to the window.

"This is not right, Lydia. I cannot stand by while you are forced into service!"

Her nose crinkled. "Jacob, what do you propose I do? Bar the doors and refuse entry to the new vicar? Nay, this has been a long time coming. I should have discussed my future with Papa when I had the chance. We knew I was not to be an heiress, so as much as I have enjoyed running his household and tutoring the local children, I am now a spinster. We should have talked about what would come next when he was no longer here. I guess we might have soon. But Papa … he always thought I would marry. He could not conceive of a world where y—someone would not claim me as their wife and mother of their children. I fear I was too complacent. There ... were men who expressed interest, but I did not encourage them when I had the opportunity."

Jacob cringed inside as he stared out the window. She had meant *him*. The vicar had thought that *he*, Jacob, would come to his senses and marry his daughter. But Jacob's dissolute way of living had damaged her chances while she waited for him to notice her, to acknowledge their deep bond. *Blast!* He was so ashamed of himself, yet simultaneously fighting back a jealous outburst. Who? Which men had expressed their interest? But he had no right to be jealous when he had left his loyal Lydia rusticating in the north while he pursued the thrills of barracks' life in the sunny south. He hated himself, the cynic he had gradually become over the last few years away from her.

"We could marry ..." he mumbled.

"What's that?"

He turned to her and spoke with resolve. "We could marry. I could provide you the protection of my name and household. It would be a good match, and it is time for me to settle down. You would make a fine wife, and I would be honored to have children with you." Not the most romantic sentiments he could express, but what did one do when his sweetheart was grieving for her father who had only just been buried? *What an awful situation.*

Lydia had gone still, her mouth hanging open in aston-ishment.

"Say yes, Lydia. We will leave immediately for the Scottish border. There is just enough time to make it there and back. On our return, I will deposit you in my grandfather's house. Sir James will be most happy to welcome a fine woman such as yourself into his household. I have to return tomorrow evening to be back at the barracks on time, but I will get leave approved to come back as soon as possible—perhaps as soon as next month—and we will make plans for our own household." He crossed the room to drop down on his knee. Reaching out, he took hold of her delicate hand, gloved in black, and raised it to his lips. "Say yes, Lydia. Say you will marry me?"

Lydia gazed at him, speechless, with troubled brown eyes, her hand trembling in his. He suspected that she had waited a long time for this proposal, and he wanted to spill words of love, the speech he had prepared on his journey home to see her. He cursed the fates for their timing and that he could not say the words in his heart without being selfish.

"What about love? Don't you want to find love?"

"Lydia, I hold you in the highest esteem. You are my best friend, and I want you to be my wife. Please say yes. I want you to say yes," he pleaded, the best he could do under these circumstances.

She blinked, a lone tear streaking down her cheek as she took a deep breath. He waited for her answer, scarcely breathing in anticipation, ready to prepare arguments to persuade her if she declined.

"Yes—yes, I will marry you!"

CHAPTER 3

LATE JUNE 1815

Four months had passed since Jacob and Lydia had returned to the village. There had barely been time for him to settle her at his grandfather's ancestral home before he had to hurry off to catch the coach. He had given her a swift kiss on her grief-numbed lips, which she had barely felt in the daze of activity, and murmured quick instructions to pack her belongings, and her father's books, and bring them to the manor. And to write to him. He had promised he would return within a month or two, as soon as he could secure leave.

However, within days of his departure, news had spread that the French dictator had escaped from the island of Elba, and by March, war had broken out. She and her new husband had been able to exchange only a couple of letters before he had departed for the Continent.

At first Lydia had felt lost, her daily routine destroyed. With too much time on her hands, she had come to regret how selfish she had been in accepting Jacob's proposal and their ill-advised trip to Gretna Green. Jacob felt an obligation to a close childhood friend, and she had taken advantage. In the heat of the moment, she had dared to hope that her unrequited love for him was … requited. However, once she had time to process her grief and to think, she had understood that he had married her out of pity. There had been no assurances of love, he was merely an honorable friend who had felt the need to protect her. Over the years, since his grandfather had purchased Jacob's commission, Lydia had suspected that there were women he had kept company with, but she had always hoped that one day he would ascertain his deep, abiding love for her and return home to court her. Months had turned into years, and by the time her father had passed away so unexpectedly, it had been clear—she had waited too long for him to notice her as a woman, and he never would.

As Lydia walked on the lane back to the manor, she breathed in the smell of summer flowers and lush greenery, struggling to focus her mind on the fields and trees to either side of her. Lamenting the past served no purpose, yet, despite this reminder, again her mind drifted to her worries. Having a family with Jacob, children of her own, had always been her deepest desire. Her marriageable years had passed her by while she had remained trapped in a love that would never be. In her mourning, his proposal had shocked her, an old dream suddenly realized, but it had only taken a week after his departure to waken from the dream and discover that in her grief she had stolen Jacob's future to fulfill her own selfish desires.

There was nothing to be done but wait for him to come home, so Lydia had returned to tutoring children in the village. It kept her busy and her mind off her trials. Trials like her self-serving acceptance of his proposal, her need—her *greed*—to finally be connected to the man she had loved since she was a child.

Walking along the lane back to the Lewises' manor, she

once again felt guilt creeping up on her. Handsome, amusing Jacob could have had any wife he wanted, but she had stolen his future in a desperate moment and she prayed he would not grow to resent her.

Her mind was overwhelmed with worry for him of late, knowing that far away her best friend fought for his life. The news of the battle at Waterloo was gruesome, and it was reported many lives had been lost. For all she knew, her husband could be fatally wounded or dead. Her body felt heavy with dread as she neared the manor, her fearful thoughts gloomy as she reached the front entrance.

Entering the dim hall, she was approached by Henry, a young redheaded footman who had joined the household at the same time as Lydia. "Mrs. Lewis, did you have a good day?"

"Yes, thank you, Henry. The Smith children made good progress in our lessons today. Did the maids manage to remove the stain in the hall?"

"Yes, Mrs. Lewis. It took some time, but Molly was able to sort it. While you were out, a missive arrived for you."

Lydia's heart leapt with excitement as she reached out for the letter on the tray. The handwriting was Jacob's. Her hands shaking, she broke open the wax seal and carefully unfolded the pages.

My dearest Lydia,

As we prepare for battle, my thoughts are consumed with our last moments together. I feel I left so much unsaid, without realizing I may never have another chance to say what is in my heart. I will return to you once this unexpected, horrible war ends, as it must, and we will have an honest, heartfelt conversation together as we did when we were children. Suffice it to say that marrying you before I left is the best decision I have ever made and the proudest moment of my life. Even in your grief, you were so beautiful it made my heart ache to behold you.

Your correspondence is the sole highlight of my time here, and I read and reread your missives so many times the pages are falling apart. Why did I not write to you more when I had the chance?

It may be some time before I can get word to you again, but every night I pray I will see you soon and that you are in good health. I will return to you, I promise, sweet princess.

Jacob

HOPE AND WORRY BLENDED TOGETHER. Lydia was uncertain if she should cry or laugh. The missive had been written some weeks earlier, but it would seem Jacob did not regret marrying her and … perhaps … he had grown as attached to her as she was to him. Feeling light with joy while weepy from worry, she hurried upstairs to change for dinner. Jacob would return home alive and well, because any other outcome was too cruel to contemplate.

* * *

DINNER in the Lewis household was an awkward affair. The baronet, Sir James, was old and frail, so he rarely left his rooms, which left Lydia to dine alone with Uncle Horace, the baronet's heir.

Uncle Horace was a man in his upper forties about the same height as Jacob, with the coppery hair and Lewis eyes. That was where similarities ended. His stringy hair was streaked with gray and his snub nose a deep rouge from excess drinking. His skin and the whites of his eyes were sallow—a startling deep shade of yellow. He was scrawny while distinctly bloated in the midriff, and he spoke only of his favorite subject—himself. In between comments about his own importance, his proficiencies and other inane chatter, Uncle Horace had the discomforting tendency to fix his watery blue eyes on her bosom. Lydia had taken to wearing shawls around the house, even on the hottest nights, to dissuade his practice of staring at her chest, but this evening was so warm she had been forced to discard it mid-dinner. She ate hurriedly, planning to plead a headache because he had not raised his eyes from her chest in at least half an hour while he drank down wine at an alarming pace.

"Girl, I couldn't find you earlier when I wanted to talk. Where were you all day?"

"I was tutoring in the village, Uncle Horace. Did you need me for something?"

"I received my new beaver from London—special delivery—along with a new suit in gold brocade I wanted to show you. Splendid, I tell you. Quite the fashion. I plan to wear it to the Stafford ball in two weeks' time. I will be the talk of the village."

Lydia had no doubt that wearing an ostentatious gold brocade suit in their small village would indeed raise plenty of gossip, but bit her tongue to prevent herself from pointing this out. "Sounds most elegant, Uncle Horace," she murmured while she spooned her soup.

"No need to call me Uncle Horace, dear. You may call me Horace."

"Oh, no, sir! I couldn't do that. It would be far too familiar." As if she needed to encourage any further intimacy with a man who was obsessed with her bodice.

She felt compassion for the man because he had been widowed several years earlier and had no children as yet. On the other hand, he was young enough to rectify matters if he took steps to curtail his debauched behavior so that a woman might accept him.

He was well on his way to being in his cups, and Lydia was never more relieved that propriety dictated no hard liquor should be consumed at the dinner table. Having reached her limit after finishing the roasted rosemary lamb, Lydia stood abruptly and, putting the back of her wrist to her temple in a show of female weakness, prepared to make her excuses about a headache.

"Sit down, girl. We still have a dessert course coming." Uncle Horace was particularly garrulous and hitting the wine harder than usual, and she was desperate to leave his company.

"If you do not mind, Uncle Horace, I feel a headache coming on and I must take my leave. I would not wish to afflict you with my unfortunate company."

He waved his hand in arrogant dismissal, and Lydia stole her cue to leave the room. Grabbing her shawl to wrap around her shoulders and conceal her bodice, she reflected that there was no dessert yet invented that would be worth suffering through any more of his inebriated company.

* * *

THE FAR-OFF TOLLING of the long-case clock declared it was midnight, stirring Lydia from her restless sleep. By the time she had reached her bedroom earlier that evening, the fabricated headache had become real, a product of her worry for Jacob and the fervent hope that he had survived the battle at Waterloo. She gazed into the darkness, her thoughts crashing like waves on a beach, while she considered what Jacob might be doing at that moment. Was he wounded? Was he alive? How could she find out, or did she have to wait in agony until he was finally able to write to her?

If he could not write to her, would someone eventually inform her of his condition?

As her thoughts chased each other back and forth, she heard the unexpected click of her door opening.

CHAPTER 4

$\mathcal{B}$ruised and battered, her chest tight with fear, Lydia rushed around her room thrusting clothes into an ancient valise, along with the heavy coin purse she had stolen. Stumbling around in the dark, she found her father's Bible and forced it into the overflowing bag, beating it all down until she could shut the clasp. Panting with anxiety, she paused to get her bearings, her swollen throat aching with every breath. She hurriedly donned a walking dress, spencer, and half walking boots before grabbing the over-stuffed valise to run from the bedroom, muffling her frantic sobs as she ran down the main stairs to the front hall.

Terrified, but trying to keep a logical mind, she made for the kitchen and quickly ferreted out bread, cheese, and apples, but realized she could not fit it all in. Calming herself, she opened her valise and repacked it carefully to make space for the food while her pulse raced in panic. *Hurry, Lydia, hurry!*

Finally, the bag was shut. It felt like it had been hours, but she knew only minutes had passed. She struggled with the kitchen door and somehow managed to get it open. Then she ran, her legs pumping while she held the valise against her heaving chest with one hand and lifted her long skirts with the other, leaving the manor behind her. She ran, away from the village where she had spent her entire life, toward the moonlit meadows to the south. And she kept running.

* * *

SEVERAL DAYS LATER, Lydia sat in the Avonmead study on the duke's elegant Chesterfield sofa of red and white striped silk. Carefully dressed—and composed—in her mourning attire, after her midnight escape from the Lewis manor, she was waiting for the gentleman to respond. Nervous perspiration dampened her palms and seconds ticked by while the Duke of Halmesbury considered all she had told him.

"You have placed a great deal of trust in me, Mrs. Lewis."

"Jacob said you always help a friend in need … I … I hoped that by extension I would be considered a friend in need, Your Grace?"

He smiled. A peer of such vaunted rank—and handsome to boot, with his thick blond curls, steady gray eyes, and warrior stature—Halmesbury should have been intimidating, but somehow the warmth of his presence made her feel safe. Safe for the first time in many days since she had begun her long, perilous journey to the south. "Princess Lydia of Thorne? You are already a friend, we just hadn't met yet."

Lydia felt a hot rush of embarrassment mixed with plea-sure. "Jacob told you about that?"

"Of course, you are exceedingly important to Captain Jacob Lewis. We spent many midnight hours swapping tales, and you always featured prominently in his."

Lydia's lips curved up, relaxing into the memories of their youth while feeling a pang in her chest when she thought of Jacob at war.

"I could escort you back to your village to seek justice in Jacob's absence, but I am sensing that is not what you want?"

She shook her head adamantly. "The baronet is frail ... an invalid ... the shock of a scandal in his household ... it might kill him. I could never do that to Jacob. He loves the old man too much for me to cause any trouble."

The duke sighed. "I was afraid you might say something like that. I will leave the matter alone, since Jacob will want to mete out retribution himself and will not appreciate it if I rob him of that privilege. I can offer you the protection of my household until Jacob returns, and I promise to protect you as if you are a member of my own family, as he would do if our positions were reversed." He looked young and vulnerable while he stared thoughtfully for a moment before he finally continued. "As it happens, you may be of help. I hate to burden you, with all you have recently experienced—"

"Please, Your Grace, it is only fair given the intimate nature of our discussion, and your offer of protection, that I hear anything you might need to discuss."

He smiled in relief. "You are indeed a vicar's daughter, Mrs. Lewis. My bride ... she is not ... adjusting well to married life. A strong, female presence—especially a married woman—would be a great boon right now. Perhaps I can offer you a position as companion?"

"I would love to help, but I must confess that the last thing I need right now is too much time on my hands to think—I fear as a companion I will go mad with my worries. Could I do something ... more active in your household while still assisting your wife?"

The duke thought for several moments. "My housekeeper is due to retire. You are eminently qualified as an educated woman, from a good family, who has run a household for many years. Hopefully your husband will forgive me for putting you into service when you tell him that it is what you wanted?"

Lydia's spirits lifted. It sounded perfect; her days would be filled with new challenges, and she had no doubt she would be safe while she waited for Jacob's return. *If he returns.*

"Yes, I would like that very much. And I would like to be discreet about my identity, since I am not sure if there will be any consequences from what happened last week?"

"I agree. What do you propose?"

"I have been traveling as Mrs. Thorne, widow of a commissioned officer. I think I would like to continue to go by that name."

He inhaled deeply while he mulled it over. "Agreed. As long as I have your assurance that you will write to Captain Lewis and let him know where he can find you when he returns."

CHAPTER 5

PRESENT DAY, OCTOBER 1818

*L*ydia's heart raced as she stared across the room at her estranged husband. When he did not come for her three years earlier, she had thought he had made his decision—to cut her loose after marrying her from a sense of misguided duty. Or, worse, that he had died in battle. Either way, she had been too afraid to find out and, after her initial letter, had never tried contacting him again. Better that she lock all the pain and loss away while staying busy.

After three years serving as the Duke of Halmesbury's housekeeper, she had decided it was time to pursue her own dreams and forge her own path. She had grown tired of waiting for her life to begin while her youth continued to slip by. It was clear that children of her own were out of the question, so the day after she turned twenty-eight, she had screwed up the courage to approach the duke about the Halmesbury Home for Children, enlightening him about the poor conditions at the Home and proposing that he undertake its improvement and appoint her the director so she could work with little ones once more. Her position in the ducal household had been challenging but not as rewarding as the time she had spent tutoring children, and she missed working with them. If she could not have her own, she could at least provide love and guidance to the orphans who needed a motherly figure in their lives.

The duke had proved enthusiastic about the idea, immediately embarking on a tour of the Home and readily agreeing to improve it. As he was now widowed himself, she observed that the project appeared to give him renewed purpose. She suspected that he, too, was feeling lonely and experiencing the yearning for family and perhaps needed the opportunity to compensate for the unborn child he had lost when his wife had passed away.

Now that she had finally found her purpose in life, closing the door on her past, Jacob would show up to confuse her thoughts.

"We can get an annulment," she finally offered in a hoarse voice.

"Annulment?" He frowned in confusion.

"We never consummated the marriage. That is grounds to seek an annulment, isn't it? I have no wish to trap you in a loveless marriage."

Jacob exploded as he stormed across the room. "You think I want an annulment? I have searched for you since I returned from that blasted war. It's been three years, and the first words out of your mouth are 'we can get an annulment'?"

Lydia backed up quickly, bumping against the wall as Jacob stopped merely inches in front of her. He raised his hands and untied her bonnet strings, casting the headpiece aside before resting his arms against the wall on either side of her head and leaning over her, his warm breath fanning her locks while his eyes turned an angry blue and glared intensely into hers. "Let's remove any grounds for annulment right now, shall we?"

With that, he lowered his head and captured her lips in their first proper kiss. Lydia was spellbound by his warm, firm lips, and they stood in stunned silence for several pulsing seconds with their mouths pressed together. Then passion unleashed without warning. Lydia threw her arms around his neck while he assaulted her lips, nipping and suckling until she moaned in desire, allowing him to steal his silky tongue into her mouth. She flinched in surprise before a wave of hot sensation overcame her and she responded in kind, matching every stroke of his tongue and pressing her body up into his hard leanness. Jacob groaned as he tore his lips away and bent down to shower kisses along the slope of her cheek and down her neck, pausing at the top of her lavender spencer to frantically tear at the buttons carved from bone. The rasp of his unshaven face against her sensitive skin sent indecent excitement racing through her pulsing veins to settle low in her belly, throbbing between her thighs.

"My God, Lydia, I have dreamed of you every night for the past four years," he muttered as he pulled the edges of the spencer apart. Hungrily, he licked her bare skin just above the modest edge of her ivory walking dress, and she melted in a pool of tingling heat, moaning and shivering her own frustrated longings. "The last thing on my mind is annulling the marriage. Nay, princess, the first thing on my mind is starting our marriage. I believe I am owed my conjugal rights, bride!"

With difficulty, Lydia pulled back and turned her head away while her hands came up to rest on his heaving chest. She pushed gently, feeling overwhelmed. Jacob immediately relented by moving back a few inches.

"I apologize," she panted, his unique smell invading her

senses with the scent of shaving soap, laundered linen, and cooling mint. "Let's talk properly. Your last letter to me, you promised we would speak on your return. That conversation is overdue."

Jacob stepped away, to her relief. His overpowering proximity was causing rippling waves of tingling desire and clouding her thoughts. She noted his breathing was as frayed as her own when he walked back across the small room, angling his front away in an odd manner, as if he was making a point of keeping his back to her. After a few moments of awkward silence, including some slight fidgeting, he responded over his shoulder, "So you did receive that letter. In the calamity of the Waterloo campaign, I was not certain. I do have to question why you never responded or wrote to tell me you had left the village?"

"I did! I did … I wrote that I was living in the duke's household and if you wished to see me you could find me there … When you didn't come, I assumed …"

"Assumed what?"

"That you regretted the wedding, that you realized it was a mistake, and that you did not wish to be burdened—"

"Lydia, you have never been a burden! Nor a mistake!" he interjected, spinning to face her in agitation. "You are my wife because I *want* you to be my wife. I scoured every inch of Yorkshire looking for you. I hired investigators, I sought out every friend and distant relation and interrogated them, but no one had any idea where you might be. The past three years have been dark—darker than being in battle. I didn't know if you were dead! It was my job to protect you, and I have been ravaged every moment of every day, imagining the worst!"

She looked at him in dazed wonder. Her persuasive, amusing Jacob who never lost his temper was currently impassioned with anger and worry. Walking over to him, she laid a gentle hand on his firm arm. "I am sorry. I should have written again. I should have realized that the letter might not make it to you. It was not my intention to cause you concern, Jacob."

The hard lines of Jacob's face relaxed as he stared down at her hand resting on his arm, which flexed in response to her touch so that her knees quaked to feel the leashed power. Lydia gazed up at his beloved face, into the murky green of his troubled eyes. "It's good to see you, Jacob. I have missed you. I have missed you like the ghost of an amputated limb. You have no idea how many times I turned around to tell you something, only to find I was alone and talking to myself."

He chuckled. "The ghost of an amputated limb? You were always fanciful … and sometimes a little macabre."

She smiled in response, and she felt her nose crinkling as it did when she teased. "That was before I started regularly reading gothic novels from the circulating library. Think of what I can imagine now with my fascination for lurid horrors encouraged to such a degree!"

* * *

JACOB'S HEART WAS FULL. Full of love, full of romantic words, full of reawakened dreams. He was intoxicated by the scent of orange blossom on soft skin and the sweet-tasting lips that had never before been explored. It was difficult to comprehend that he was standing in the same room with his beloved wife whom he had searched for these past three years, demented by the loss of her. Finally. He had to suppress the urge to pinch himself to ensure this was not yet another blissful dream from which he would awaken into a living nightmare of cold reality.

From the moment he had left his bride on his grandfather's doorstep, there had not been a moment's peace for him. He had wanted so desperately to return to her, to claim his wedding night, to make up for lost time and be like any ordinary couple, but instead he had received orders and been sent to war. For their entire marriage, the two of them had been moving in opposite directions. Now they finally stood together in the same room, an unprecedented event in which they were connected in both time and space.

Taking up her hand in his, he said, "Lydia, I wanted to marry you. More than you know. But … your father …"

"I know." She raised her other hand to cover his, squeezing gently. "I am glad you found me. I was hiding in plain sight so that you could when you wanted to."

He snorted. "Not plain enough. You have been clear on the other side of the country. Thank the Lord that *The Gentleman's Magazine* saw fit to publish that article. Now that we are reunited, what will it take for you to leave with me and return home?"

Lydia abruptly pulled her dainty hands from his and wandered over to the blue settee framed in mahogany, her face averted. He felt the keen loss of her touch and wanted to follow her, ravish her, cover her lithe body with his and make her his wife in truth. Watch her chocolate brown eyes shine with passion, breathe in the floral scent of her hair, and bury himself in her sweet, innocent warmth.

She took a seat, sitting primly on the edge, her head tilted down. Minutes passed without comment, and Jacob felt the peace of the moment slipping out of his grasp like water through his fingers.

"Lydia?"

* * *

Lydia's heart was breaking. She wanted to join Jacob, to be his wife, discover the joys of marriage … and of the marriage bed … with the man she had dreamed of for more than ten years. But how could she ask the man she loved to choose between her and his family? She couldn't even be sure he loved her. Clearly he cared, he wanted her, but there had been no words of love.

If she went with him, she would have to tell him what happened. And if she told him what happened, she would force him to make choices, potentially take actions that he would regret. She could not be responsible for tearing her beloved Jacob's world apart, like a fragile sheet of paper shredded into tiny pieces before being tossed into a roaring fire. There would be no turning back, no undoing her words. Just pain and terrible, heartbreaking decisions to make.

It would be better to let matters remain as they were. He could seek an annulment. She would be the villain and refuse to reconcile in order to save him—to ensure he would never be hurt.

"I can't … can't return with you. I have built a life here. Too much time has passed, and one can't revisit the past. We have both moved on with our lives, and we should … keep going forward. You probably have grounds for annulment, and we can end this as if it never started. Because it truly never did." As she finished speaking, she was alarmed to find her fingers, her heart, her lips all encased in ice. Freezing her to the bone. She could not look at him. She could speak no more words. It felt like her soul was withering and dying within her cold form.

Jacob inhaled sharply behind her. "Again with the annulment?" he demanded incredulously.

She gave a curt nod; it was all she could manage without breaking down.

"This is not over!" he bellowed, striding from the room

and slamming the door behind him. Lydia jumped in surprise and gazed in wooden despair at her tightly inter-locked fingers. While she listened to his heavy retreating footsteps, she consoled herself. *You have done the right thing. You have no choice.*

*J*acob made it all the way to the street corner, fuming at her stubborn resistance, cursing her obstinance and refusal to accept him, before slowly coming to his senses as slow, fat drops of rain pummeled his head. He had just found his missing wife, and he was letting his temper get the better of him. His shoulders slumped in defeat as he accepted that he had to swallow his pride to sort this out and get to the truth. His reactions did not signify; he had to choose to be calm in order to resolve this matter.

If he did not, he realized with dawning horror, she might pick up and disappear again, and he would return to a hell of his own making—forced to search for her yet again with no clues to lead his way. Fate had favored him with the article in *The Gentleman's Magazine*, or he would never have guessed she was living under an assumed name clear across the country at the estate of his old school chum.

Cooling his blood, he scowled sightlessly at the weathered cobblestones under his boots, spattered with intermittent drops of water, and fought for a logical state of mind. It took only a few seconds to recall that his Lydia was loyal and steadfast. Good Lord, she had waited years for him to come up to scratch. She did not do stupid, unpredictable things like disappear into the night, never to resurface. She had left her entire life behind: her friends, the children she tutored, her father's book collection … him … and their love.

Something had happened. Something was wrong, and he had failed to get to the root of the problem. The young woman he grew up with was reliable and never driven by capricious impulses. *Why had Lydia run away and changed her name?*

Blowing a hard puff of air, he stood on the corner, breathing in the smell of fresh rain and racking his brain for any clues. Had she said anything that would explain her sudden disappearance?

Feeling embarrassed by his tantrum, he turned and walked back down the street and climbed the stone steps to her red-painted door. Letting himself in, he continued on to the front room. His wife needed him, and he would do whatever it took to gain her trust.

* * *

LYDIA FLINCHED in dismay when Jacob re-entered the room, her resolve strained. She wanted to blurt out what had really happened, why she had run away, but she could not. Staring into the cold hearth, she vowed to not spew the truth and ruin Jacob's life, thus forcing him to choose between his wife and his family.

Coming over to her, he settled down before her on one knee with the other propped up to lean his elbow on. His hair glistened with errant raindrops while he stared down at the floor before giving a deep sigh, lifting his shoulders and chest with the force of his breath.

"I promised you that when I returned, I would share the words not spoken the day I proposed to you, so … I won't lie, Lydia. I *can* live without you. I had to live without you for over three years. But the truth is, without you I am merely alive, a shell of a man. It is not truly living, it is merely surviving, because … without you there is nothing to look forward to. Life is an endless progression of putting one foot in front of the other. With you, life is glorious with infinite possibilities and boundless dreams. Every day brings new meaning, and each moment is filled with excitement and imagination. It always has been this way, and finding you … my soul is reawakened. Wherever you are, that is where my heart is. I did not marry you out of duty, princess, I married you because you were—and *are*—a vital component of my life and I had come to realize just how much I loved you as the woman who completes me."

He paused to press a large, tanned hand over her tightly clasped fingers. Lydia's chin quivered as she fought for control over her emotions, barely daring to breathe as Jacob continued. "I regret all the years I made you wait while I acted out some ridiculous coming-of-age parody—the so-called need to sow my wild oats. None of it was necessary. I was lucky enough to have the real thing right in front of me my entire youth, and I squandered our years together. If I had behaved differently, we would not be in these current circumstances and whatever drove you away would never have happened. I accept full responsibility for my actions, and from the bottom of my heart, I apologize for being a foolish idiot."

Lydia felt hot tears spilling over her cheeks. Mortified by her loss of composure, she choked back a sob. Jacob raised his head, his face falling at the sight of her tears. "No, sweet princess, please do not cry." Swooping her into a tight embrace, Jacob pressed kisses to her hair, which made her sob louder, the walls coming down and her broken soul bared before him.

"It won't work, Jacob! We cannot turn back," she sobbed, desperate to send him away. "We had our chance and it was not meant to be. *We* were not meant to be! You must accept this and leave."

He shushed her cries while he continued to embrace her, running his large hands up over her shoulders and down her back and refusing to let her go. She dissolved in a storm of tears, crying for what could have been, the dreams of her youth, and that even with Jacob here, he had never been more unattainable.

"It won't work, Jacob! You must leave and forget you found me! There are no circumstances in which I will return with you and we pretend none of this happened—"

"I am not going anywhere, love. You will have to tell me why you left … what happened? Why were you forced to leave?"

"I wanted a change of scenery. My father had passed away, and the grief was eating away at me!"

"I don't believe you, princess. Try telling me the truth."

"I felt gut-wrenching guilt over marrying you. I shouldn't have put you in that position!"

"Deep down you always knew I loved you. You always knew that our marriage was the only possible outcome to our story. Tell me the true reason you left, my love."

The comfort of his embrace was too much to bear. Lydia rested her head against his muscular shoulder, hugging him tightly as a wave of traumatic memories bore down on her— that night, the decision to leave it all behind … to leave *him* behind, the perilous journey to Halmesbury, the letter she had written to him, waiting for a reply that never arrived. It was all too much to handle at once; the turmoil was crushing in its volume. She gave in.

CHAPTER 7

LATE JUNE 1815 AT MIDNIGHT

She heard the unexpected click of her door opening. Half asleep and a little confused, at first she thought that Jacob had returned from the war when she saw the tall form standing in the doorway, the dim light casting him in shadows. But when she blinked, her vision cleared and she saw that the figure was too bloated around the waist, the shoulders too bent and scrawny to be her athletic, soldier husband. Scrambling into a seated position, her heart pounded and her blood ran cold as she realized that Uncle Horace was invading her bedchamber.

"Get out!" she yelped, pulling the brocade counterpane firmly up to her neck.

"I don't think so, lovely Lydia."

"Jacob will kill you if you do not leave this room!"

"You invited me!"

"What—"

"You removed your shawl at dinner to tempt me with your fine, young form."

"It was sweltering and I was afraid I would faint if I did not—"

Uncle Horace ignored her as he staggered into the room. "For all intents and porpoises … porpoises? Yes, for all intents and porpoises, I am the head of this household, and I am claiming my *droit du seigneur*—the right of the lord to spend the first night in the bride's bed. I assume there was no wedding night?" Lydia flushed in humiliation, but he did not wait for her to answer. "No matter if there was, I will take you anyway. You would do well to keep me happy when your husband likely lies dead under a pile of rotting carcasses. I hear more than ten thousand Englishmen lost their lives and they are still counting the bodies. Soon you will rely holy … holy? No, *wholly* on my generosity, so it would behoove you to be nice."

It would have been laughable how inebriated he was if she hadn't been terrified out of her wits. Lydia threw the covers aside and scrambled over the bed away from Uncle Horace as he approached her, but lost her balance when a meaty hand grabbed her by the ankle and hauled her back. Even deep in his cups, the man was strong—too strong. His weight crushed her into the mattress and tangled bedding, and she struggled against him in panic but he quickly over-powered her, turning her over to wrap his sweaty, bloated hand around her throat while she fought for air. His brandy-soaked breath fanned her face in heavy gusts, and she realized the drunkard was beyond reason as he ran his other large, grasping hand over her breasts to violently squeeze.

Frantic, her free hand flayed out, searching—searching for anything to help her free herself while her vision grew spotty as she started to lose consciousness. Grasping in desperation, her fingers touched the edge of her father's Bible. Sucking in a wheezing breath of relief, she pulled at it until it was firmly in hand, then lifted it behind Uncle Horace's despicable head, fear fueling her with the strength she needed to bring the heavy book crashing down on the base of his skull.

He immediately slumped, crushing her chest but releasing her throat. For a second, Lydia lay in stunned silence, drawing reedy breath through her swollen throat before squirming and wiggling to get out from under the man's deadweight. Horror set in when she barely moved an inch, his heavy form too much mass for her to shift. She paused to calm herself, finding it difficult to draw breath into her lungs with his torso crushing her chest. She needed to use her mind to calculate the physics of the situation and then employ all her intention to the solution in a focused burst of applied effort. Drawing her strength and resolve, she worked out the best leverage. Resolutely, she wiggled and tugged in a concerted effort to extricate her pinned arm, determined in her terror of an enraged Horace regaining consciousness while she lay trapped beneath him.

Once both arms were free, she placed her hands against the top of his shoulder and strained with every ounce of strength she possessed, and some extra strength that she did not possess except in her imagination, bearing down on his shoulder and clavicle in order to push her body back and sideways. Once she had freed several inches of her upper torso, she sucked in much-needed air for several moments until she was able to resume the wiggling in short bursts. After several minutes of digging in her heels and sliding up and sideways, then resting before moving again, she finally tore herself loose of his unconscious body.

Sitting on the bed next to him, catching her breath, she picked up the heavy tome once more and brought the flat side down on the back of his head for good measure. Just to be sure. And to give her time to think.

She rose unsteadily from the bed, sending a furtive prayer of gratitude to her father for the use of his Good Book in saving herself. Lydia gathered her scrambled thoughts to plan out what to do next. Approaching the elderly baronet to tell him what happened was out of the question; his health was fading and the scandal would severely distress him. If it caused his decline or death, Lydia would be at the full mercy of Uncle Horace's notions of his feudal rights or *droit du seigneur*, as he called them. And she might rob Jacob of the opportunity to see his grandfather once more.

Nay, she had been selfish enough wedding her heart's desire. She needed to run. And hide because she had assaulted the heir of a baronetcy. An important man, and men were always forgiven their little foibles, while as a woman … as a woman she could and would be held to blame for enticing him. The scandal would be devastating—for her, not him—but worse, she might be arrested for a grievous assault on his person.

CHAPTER 8

PRESENT DAY, OCTOBER 1818

While Lydia related the story of her departure, Jacob had become agitated. Midway through, he had released her from their embrace to light a fire in the hearth. The warm glow heated her ice-cold fingers as she concluded the tale, then waited.

He rubbed his hands over his face, breathing rapidly while he appeared to struggle with fierce control over himself. Finally, he looked at her, his eyes a deep green with strong emotion. Her husband was two hundred pounds of angry male. Lydia blinked in consternation.

"I will kill him! I will dig him up from his grave and kill him all over again!"

"His *grave*? I swear he was breathing when I left!"

"You did not kill him—he was very much alive when I returned from war. But one thing at a time. I am so, so sorry. I am so sorry! I can't believe you were trying to protect me— my grandfather—when I should have protected you." Jacob had fallen to his knees in front of her and buried his face in her skirts. Hesitantly, Lydia raised a trembling hand to hover.

Then brought it down to caress his crisp, copper curls in comfort.

"Jacob, it was a long time ago. I survived it. And you did the best you could. You married me and gave me shelter in your family home. You could never have predicted what would happen, and you were fighting for your life—and those of your men—on foreign soil. I don't blame you. I never blamed you."

"You don't need to—I blame myself. I knew he was a profligate drunkard. I should have taken measures!"

"Sweet Jacob, this is why I did not tell you. I did not want to torment you, to make you choose between your family and myself. But, my love, what is this about a grave?" she asked with trepidation.

"Uncle Horace is no longer with us."

"He is dead?"

"Yes. I returned from France in October of that year and was arranging to sell my commission. I had seen so much death ... I did not want to take a chance on being sent to war a second time. More importantly, I never wanted to be forced apart from you again and following the drum is no life for a woman. I came home to find you were missing. Uncle Horace said perhaps you had run off with another man, which, of course, made no sense ... One night, we attended a dinner at the Jamisons' and Uncle Horace disappeared. The men were gathered in the billiard room when we heard Mrs. Jamison screaming blue murder. Her husband raced out to find Uncle Horace, in a drunken stupor, trying to assault his wife out in the hall. My uncle ran off into the night, with Mr. Jamison giving chase and threatening to kill him. The wicked, drunken idiot ran into the woods between our two homes and vanished. Two days later, we found him in a ravine where he must have stumbled and hit his head on a rock. It appeared he had bled out over several hours, for the ground was steeped in blood."

"I-I'm so sorry."

"It was hell. Grandfather was so frail by that time; I could not find it in me to tell him that his heir had died … and under such scandalous circumstances. I simply waited and never told him."

"Never told him … did Sir James pass on?"

"He did."

"But-but that makes you a baronet!"

"Indeed, Lady Lewis."

Lydia shook her head in denial. "You are not serious!"

"You are officially a lady. But to me, you will always be my princess."

Lydia was dazed by the news. There was no family and no potential scandal. Jacob did not need to choose sides. *And they could be together!*

Then reality came crashing down. She had responsibilities, children depending on her, the Home that needed her. She couldn't just leave it all behind. Her heart dropped.

"What is it? You look like you lost your favorite book."

"I can't leave Halmesbury. I have built a life here. People—children—depend on me!"

He clasped her cold hands in his large, warm ones, rubbing heat into her frozen digits. "Lydia, I am immensely proud of you. You have endured some terrible trials, yet have found the courage to persist through it all. I should not have suggested that you abandon all you have achieved through your hard work and on your own merit and simply walk away. My love, you have waited years for me, and now we will follow your dreams—*together*—because I am eternally grateful that you have granted me the honor of your precious love."

"But how will that work—what will we do?"

"We will figure it out. Perhaps over time you may choose to relinquish some of your duties to others, but that can be a gradual process and at your discretion. I am sure I can find investments or philanthropic endeavors to occupy me here in the south, as long as we can travel to our village every few months. I have a highly competent steward who has been running the estate for some years, and I can manage my obligations through the post for the majority of the year."

"You would do that for me?" She felt a surge of hope returning.

"I would do anything for you. And the truth is that I would go mad rusticating as the baronet of a tiny village. I only stayed there to await your return, and I need a greater purpose than that. Halmesbury is a fine town, and I prefer the south of England anyhow, if I am being honest."

Lydia groaned, hanging her head in renewed agony. "Everyone knows me as the widow, Mrs. Thorne! How can I stay here and explain why I now have a husband and my name is Lady Lewis? It can't be borne, it is all so complicated! Why did I not think this through when I chose a false name and then moved into town to run a children's home? What was I thinking?"

Jacob huffed in suppressed laughter, unable to conceal his amusement. He took the seat next to her and drew her into his arms. She nestled against his chest as he dropped his chin to rest on her head.

"How about we feign a courtship while I find us a proper home to live in, one where we might be able to start a family, and in a few weeks, we pretend to wed? That will explain your change in name, and we will hope that no one from our village ever comes to Halmesbury to reveal we were already married. If they do, we will laugh it off as eccentric behavior of the gentry and continue on with our lives. There is no scandal here, just complexity."

"We can do that?"

"I will visit the duke and work it out. I am certain he will assist. And, in the meanwhile, I can court you properly as I should have done, and we can look forward to an improper wedding followed by a proper wedding night. You deserve the gestures of courtship, the admiration of your beau. You are a singular woman, and I owe it to you to make you feel appreciated and admired. Say yes, my love, and I will make it happen."

"I will," she intoned, echoing their wedding vows and causing Jacob to chuckle. As she rested against his broad shoulder, she listened to the rhythm of his heartbeat and closed her eyes in bliss, at long last finding her way into the arms of her beloved.

EPILOGUE

I t was a cool, crisp morning in early December when Jacob's curricle came to a stop in the front drive of Avonmead. The Duke of Halmesbury had a fine ancestral estate with lush parklands dotted with grazing sheep and trees lightly bedecked with the last remaining autumn-colored leaves. Lydia's "betrothed" alighted and turned to help her out. When her feet hit the ground, she looked up at the manor that had been her home for several years. The Palladian front was a gorgeous honeyed stone with symmetrical staircases converging under a portico with impressive, carved front doors. She found herself looking at the manor with fresh eyes—those of a bride to a baronet.

Jacob tucked her arm in his, and they made their way up the stone steps to the front door. Her husband had courted her for several weeks, taking her on drives, visiting tea rooms, and showering her with gifts of flowers and books. Her colleagues and acquaintances had expressed their admiration of his handsome appearance and excellent connections while he had made good on his promise to give her the attentions of an honorable courtship. Her self-doubt had healed as it became clear that her husband truly admired and loved her, and that a sense of duty was not the cornerstone of their newfound affinity.

Shortly they were shown into the duke's large, unusual library. A sizable wall of small-paned windows revealed the parklands and an expanse of cloudy sky framed by a lattice of wooden arches, with a great medallion at the crest. The library included two stories of leather-bound books with a spiral staircase leading to the second-floor landing. The grand room had a distinct North African flavor to the architectural features and furnishings due to the travels of the Markham ancestors.

The tall, blond duke bowed in greeting and his lovely bride, the new duchess, stepped forward to grasp Lydia's hands in her own. "Mrs. Thorne, it is such a pleasure to host you this morning!"

Within a few months of Lydia joining the ducal household three years earlier, the duke had suffered his own loss when his first wife had died of a fever within months of their marriage, along with their unborn child. The duke and Lydia had grieved in tandem for their lost loves, forging a personal bond in their mutual casualties. However, just a few weeks before Jacob had shown up on her doorstep, Lydia had heard that the duke had unexpectedly married the lively young daughter of a Somerset baron. His bride had turned out to be a vivacious, kind beauty, and it warmed her heart to see the duke looking so lighthearted and in love, for there was no man more deserving than he.

Behind them, the door clicked shut when the first footman left the room. The duke gestured to the lugubrious vicar perched on the edge of a reclining couch of green Morocco leather, his hands primly folded over a Book of Common Prayer. "I explained your unusual circumstances to the vicar and, although he is not willing to lie about a wedding ceremony taking place, he has agreed that we will enjoy a pleasant visit in the library while he reads the wedding vows to himself quietly. After an appropriate amount of time, we will leave the room and loudly congratulate you, Sir Jacob, and you, Lady Lewis, on your marriage, with no mention of when this esteemed event actually occurred, so it will appear to be the reason that my wife and I, with a vicar, were in attendance in the library. We will adjourn to enjoy a wedding breakfast joined by my wife's brother, and some of the servants would like to congratulate you on the implied festivities. If the vicar is asked anything about this morning's—ahem—*event*, he has agreed to be evasive and change the subject. By all appearances, a wedding will have taken place this morning, rather than nearly four years ago, and you will leave Avonmead publicly as husband and wife."

Lydia felt the threat of tears thickening her throat. She could not believe that everyone was going to so much trouble for her and Jacob. The young duchess, her luscious chestnut hair coiffured into trailing curls around her face, piped in. "It won't hold up to close scrutiny, since there will be no record of a common license at the church, nor of a wedding, but we think it will suffice as there is no reason for anyone to be curious or question the matter."

Lydia smiled in gratitude at the happy couple while Jacob stepped forward to shake the duke's hand. They slapped a hand against each other's shoulder in mutual friendship as Jacob spoke gruffly. "Thank you, Your Grace. There are no words to express my appreciation for keeping my wife safe in my absence."

"Think nothing of it. Mrs. Thorne—Lady Lewis—added great value to my household, and I am inordinately grateful for her presence here the past three years. I am only regretful that it meant the two of you were parted for far too long.

Now … shall we enjoy this tea that is laid out and talk while we wait the appropriate amount of time for a false wedding ceremony to take place?" He gestured toward the seating area.

They went to seat themselves in library chairs inlaid with brass, surrounding a low table with a tea service laid out. And there, among an infinite number of pungent leather books, an eerie echo of the day Jacob had proposed their mad-dash wedding at Gretna Green, Lydia relaxed with a china cup and saucer in her hands, releasing a deep sigh of pure contentment and breathing in the fragrance of Twinings tea. She had looked forward to her wedding day with Jacob since she was a young girl and finally, today, her dreams were coming to fruition—she would leave the manor with him at her side. They were, at long last, coming together as man and wife.

* * *

LATER THAT DAY, in the final hours of daylight, Lydia stood on stone steps looking up at the charming terrace house Jacob had obtained in the heart of Halmesbury, close to her beloved Home. The honey-colored stone edifice invited one closer, while the large, curved sash windows promised well-lit interiors to be found once she stepped through the freshly painted door. Her second-time groom hurried her inside as he promised her that their new housekeeper, cook, and servants would be absent until the following day.

"I want you all to myself tonight, so I have arranged a meal in the kitchen to tide us over until morning."

"I am embarrassed that you had to take care of this—our new home and the hiring of servants—without me."

"Not at all, love. You did not expect my arrival, and your work and your fortunate foundlings needed your attention. I enjoyed preparing our home for us and had the time to do so."

Lydia nodded as she peered around the hall at the iron balustrades and chandelier hanging high above their heads. She had no time to notice any other details before Jacob ushered her into the front room. She burst out laughing when she crossed the threshold. On every surface of the room, even the chairs and sofa, were piles of precariously stacked books. A row of packing crates below the large windows facing onto the street were stacked with books, as was the marble mantelpiece of the fireplace. "What is this?"

"Take a look, my love."

She wandered into the room to a table set with four stacks of books of various heights and opened a red leather volume before gasping in surprise. "My father's books?" she exclaimed as she spun her head to question her husband. Jacob smiled, adoration in his gleaming turquoise eyes while he took in her delight.

"I sent for them as soon as we agreed we would live in Halmesbury."

Lydia was silent as she fought back tears of joy, lifting her arms in supplication. She knew his jest was intended to remind her of the day he had proposed and then rushed her overnight to the Scottish border.

Interpreting her signal, he walked straight into her embrace, enveloping her against his chest. "Thank you ... thank you for finding me. Thank you for wanting me. Thank you ... for loving me," she whispered.

"Princess, I can't help it. You are so irresistible ... and lovable. I only regret I was such an idiot for so long and waited until it was almost too late to make you my wife."

"Nay, no regrets. We had many adventures apart, and now we have found our way back to each other. Think of all the stories we can share now. We will relearn about each other's lives, and it will make us stronger now that we appreciate that life is better together."

"Hmm … you were always the wise one, love. However, all those years imagining this … um … wedding night, all I want to do is take you upstairs to our bedroom and finally make good on my promise to consummate our marriage vows."

Leaning her forehead against his broad shoulder, Lydia nodded against him. He eagerly swept her into his strong arms as if she were as light as a pillow filled with feathers and carefully exited into the corridor. There he climbed the stairs swiftly, taking them two at a time until they reached the first level before slowing down. "I will show you our new home, but not right now, if that is all right?"

"Please take me to bed," she agreed. Needing no further encouragement, Jacob ascended the stairs to the second landing and walked them through an open door to set her on her feet.

"I haven't bought rugs yet, and the house came with only basic furnishings. I wanted you to be involved in setting up our home. There is a dressing room through that door, and the housekeeper has unpacked your things earlier today. I hope that … you are not disappointed?" Her husband appeared a little anxious while he waited for her response.

Lydia looked around the room. A four-poster bed, carved with intricate strapwork, dominated one wall. A crude packing crate was positioned next to it, intended as a makeshift dressing table. The oak floor was bare of rugs, and no other furnishings were to be seen. Even the windows were mostly bare, with a simple swath of muslin draped over them. Her lips slowly curved up as she envisioned filling their home with treasures together.

"It's perfect."

* * *

"Nay, wife, *you are perfect*." Taking hold of her upper arm, Jacob gently swung her around to wrap his arms around her. Resting his cheek on her thick sable locks, he went utterly still. He soaked in the exquisite joy of holding his princess, his Lydia, in his arms, feeling her soft, womanly body pressed into the hard edges of his own. Breathing in the orange blossom fragrance of her hair, listening to her deep breathing and feeling the rise and fall of her breasts against his lower chest in quiet accompaniment. He had dreamed of making love to her before they even married, knowing it would transcend any sexual experiences of his past because he would be lying with the most honorable, sweet, clever, imaginative woman he had ever encountered. The only woman he had ever loved. He had lost so much time with her that now he had no choice but to savor every slow, ticking second of their first night together ... of every night they shared together.

His blood thickened and heat spread from his limbs to center in his groin while he captured every pulsing sense of this moment. Slowly he turned his head to breathe against her vulnerable temple, his pulse increasing as his body attuned to hers in perfect rhythm. Combing his fingers through her silky locks elicited a purr of pleasure from her rose-pink lips, shooting ecstasy along his nerve endings to gather at his groin.

He cupped the back of her head, his large hand engulfing her delicate skull, and tilted her to steal his lips against hers in a fleeting graze. She stirred in response before he took possession of her lips, licking and nipping to gather the sweetness before coaxing her lips apart to plunge his tongue in an aching, hungry exploration of her mouth. Dying in hardening pleasure when her tongue sought and tentatively explored his in return.

One of his hands worked between them, and he deftly undid the frogs of her spencer. He moved as he continued to lick at her lips, taking the edges in hand and pushing it off her shoulders, and then slowly down her arms until the weight of it dropped to the floor. Gently grabbing her hand, he raised it to press his lips against her inner wrist where her pulse beat like a startled rabbit. He blew gently on the damped spot before slowly tonguing her pulse point.

* * *

LYDIA'S HEART pounded loudly as she melted in a vortex of sensation. She had dreamed of being in Jacob's arms for so many years, until she had eventually accepted it would never be. Then he had come to her after her father's untimely death, and her buried wishes had reemerged to taunt her in her dreams—and any other moment she was foolish enough to leave her mind unoccupied. After she had escaped to Halmesbury, her yearning had slowly died as weeks turned into months, and then months into years, until she knew without a doubt that she would live her life without a single kiss from the man she had loved her entire youth. The kind of kiss a woman received from her lover ... her love.

Yet here she was, against all odds, about to share her bed with her husband who was now a permanent part of her life. All the trials, all the obstacles had been overcome and her true destiny was realized, here in Jacob's arms. Her senses were swimming, her head falling back in ecstasy as he pressed slow, searing kisses from her wrist up to her elbow and then along her upper arm to her clavicle, which was when she realized he had loosened her bodice and it was falling down. He eagerly pushed the dress down and over her hips so it draped in a heap on the wooden floor around her ankles. His hands worked quickly to loosen the tapes of her stays, which were pushed down her arms and dropped to the floor before she could inhale her next breath. His mouth sought the peak of a turgid nipple pushing against the linen of her chemise, and she realized she was mostly naked except for her thin under-garment and stockings. Murmuring her surprise, Jacob responded by raising his head to capture her lips while he scooped her up in his arms once more, striding quickly over to the bed to lay her down gently on the counterpane.

"Lydia, my wife, my love, you are so beautiful ... I have dreamed of this ... so many nights ... I can't believe—" Jacob's mumblings were interrupted by deep, drugging kisses, and Lydia could barely hear him as hot sensation shot through her, sending a tide of gooseflesh tingling down her entire body all the way to her ankles. The intimate place between her thighs throbbed, pulsing in anticipation of his hard inva-sion as his hand found the hem of her chemise and he swiftly yanked it up and over her head. She was naked before her husband, except for her stockings and garters. Slowly, modesty stole into her awareness as she pressed her legs together and brought up her arms.

"No!" He caught her arms and gently laid them out, bent on either side of her head. His eyes had turned an intense blue while he scanned her form ravenously. "My God, Lydia, you are more beautiful than any woman I have ever seen!" Cringing, his gaze shot back up to her face. "Oh princess, I didn't mean to bring up my past indiscr—"

"Jacob, I love you."

He froze, his eyes changed back to turquoise as his pupils dilated and he swallowed hard. "Say it again."

"Jacob, I love you."

His face softened as he lowered himself over her and took

her swollen lips gently with his. "And I love you, princess. With all my heart." He pulled back up to stand, yanking at his cravat, then his tailcoat and waistcoat, which he threw aside in his haste. He unfastened his shirt, then pulled it over his head and tossed it away. Lydia licked her lips when he revealed his naked torso, paler than his tanned face and hands but so exquisitely sculpted. His shoulders were broad and defined, his stomach flat except for ridges of muscle that spoke to his active life. Coppery brown hair dusted the broad musculature of his chest, before tapering down to plunge into his pantaloons. Lydia hissed in pleasure, and her hand lifted toward him. He immediately returned to lean over her. Reverently, she skated her fingertips through the matting of hair on his warm, hard body, drawing a groan from deep within his throat as she traced the battle scars across his right shoulder. She could feel their hearts beating in sweating unison, as desire and affection melted into a haze of ravenous lust.

Jacob leaned down to capture her hard nipple, suckling and scraping lightly with his teeth as she arched in mindless pleasure, her hand holding his head to her breast. A large, warm hand scraped down her side, curving in to sweep over her belly and come to rest between her legs, idly skimming her thatch of curls. She moaned loudly as her legs fell open in invitation and he swept over the seam of her sex. Nudging up, she pleaded with her body for him to close in, to touch her more intimately, but he teased and passed over without mercy until she squirmed and moaned in ecstatic frustration.

"Patience, love, I need to prepare you." She groaned in protest, tugging at his hand. "Princess, do you know what to expect?"

Lydia opened her eyes to glare at him in outrage. "I'm a worldly, well-read woman of eight-and-twenty who ran a large noble household filled with male and female servants in close proximity. Of course, I know what to expect."

Jacob's mouth tightened and he looked like he was suppressing amusement, irritating Lydia into attempting to shut her thighs. He quickly positioned himself between her legs to stop the motion, his hard length pushing against her sex and distracting her with wild longing. "My mistake, wife. I just want to confirm … no disrespect intended … but with all your vast knowledge of carnal relations, you do know that the first time hurts?"

"What?"

"The first time, it hurts for a woman. It could be slight discomfort, or more intense, but it will only hurt the first time."

Lydia was disconcerted. Her body craved his, but no one had informed her to expect this. She had grown up the only daughter of a widowed vicar, and although she knew the goings-on belowstairs as the person who had to keep the maids in hand, she had never discussed conjugal matters with anyone before. Huffing, she muttered resentfully, "Well … let's get it over with, then."

Jacob was clearly repressing a smile when he pressed his forehead into her shoulder, and she could hear him fighting back a chuckle. After an interminable time, he had composed himself to respond in a muffled voice, "Nay, my sweet wife, it will be better for you if we take our time."

He rolled to one side, and his hand returned between her legs to gently sweep over her, back and forth until her nerve endings were screaming, then he finally dipped a finger into the seam of her cleft to trail slowly upward, brushing the crest to cascade a thousand sparkles of sensation in every direction. Gasping, she lifted her hips to find his evasive fingertip while he stroked down and up again to tease her nub. Instinct drove her to pump against his hand, and he finally took pity by pressing the heel over her stimulated center, sliding a finger inside her slick, tight channel. She felt how slick her channel had become and wondered in awe about all of the unknown aspects of carnal relations before mindlessly sinking into the ecstasy of his palm rhythmically grinding against her nub as he gently thrust his finger in and out of her entrance. The pleasure built up in waves and distantly she heard herself keening, her legs splayed to seek the best angle, and white-hot sensation struck as she peaked into shattering abandon.

Slowly the pleasure receded, leaving her satiated and wrung out. She languidly opened her eyes to stare sightlessly at the ceiling while her panting died down into steady breathing. She felt Jacob release her and rise from the bed. He removed his boots and pantaloons with alacrity, shoving his small clothes off. She turned her head to look at him—he was glorious. All sculpted muscle, and tall, hard power. Her interest was drawn down to his appendage, which stood proudly erect from dark curls shielding the vulnerable weights suspended below. "You are magnificent," she uttered in astonishment.

Jacob growled as he returned to the bed, placing his knees between her legs and leaning over to invade her mouth in a searing kiss. With one hand, he reached down to grasp his length and stroked his blunt tip against her slick seam, causing her to flinch in ecstasy when he grazed her over-sensitized pearl. Gradually, he pressed his cock into her quivering channel, sliding in an inch and retreating, over and over again until she couldn't bear it, aroused to new heights by his teasing onslaught. "Please!" she cried out.

With great care he settled against her, groaning as he kissed her lips. "My apologies, princess." With that, he rushed into her, invading her tight, clenching muscles until their hips met.

Lydia gasped in dismay as her intimate muscles gave way to his invasion. Panting, they both held still while she grew accustomed to his thick length. As her body steadily untensed, he held himself over her, growling as she relaxed against him. Tentatively, she craned her head up and pressed a kiss to his sweat-misted cheek, gyrating her hips against his. Jacob was obviously struggling for control as he eased back and forth, the slow drag of his shaft heating her blood and exciting her anew. Frantic, she moved herself up and down against him, at which point his control snapped, and he plunged in and out of her as she threw her head back and screamed her delight at their joining. Jacob hit his peak, his length spasming wildly inside her as he spent into her with a loud groan, arching up into a pose of frozen triumph.

His lungs shuddered with the effort to draw air before he gently fell to one side of her and pulled her into his arms. "Lydia, my sweet, that was—was transcendent, my darling." He hugged her tight, and his kisses landed against the crown of her head like raindrops in a storm.

She lay panting in his arms, happiness permeating every cell of her body, unable to believe she had just made love to the man of her childhood—and adulthood—dreams and that he was, at long last, all hers.

AUTHOR'S NOTE

When Jacob informs Lydia that Uncle Horace bled out after hitting his head in the forest, what they would not have known when he recounted this tale was that excessive drinking can cause thinning of the blood which prevented Horace's wound from clotting. Not only did Uncle Horace suffer from alcoholism that drove him to extremes beyond acceptable behavior, it rendered him jaundiced and his body incapable of healing in order to save his life. However, this did not excuse his behavior, for each choice was his own to make, including the choice to abuse alcohol in the first place, and at any time he could have taken steps to change his ways.

Watching someone in the advanced stages of alcoholism is a tragedy to witness and leaves a lasting impression on one's thoughts. Fortunately, I have been privileged to witness the strength of character it takes to regain control of a life and see the indomitable spirit of a person fighting from the depths of illness and despair to rise like a phoenix from the ashes as a sober, contributing member of society, which leaves an indelible impression. Uncle Horace succumbed to temptation, but every day there are brave souls who take responsibility to regain their lives.

In regards to Jacob's changing eye color, I do not have a scientific explanation to provide. This character trait is based on my personal experience. Growing up with my sister, one never knew what color her eyes would appear to be as they changed with her mood in a startling range of colors from gray to hazel.

In this tale, I wanted to portray two people who were strong alone but even stronger together. A sense of duty and trying circumstances can throw a wrench into a marriage, but remaining loyal and persevering until reunited can overcome even the dreaded long-distance relationship if their bond is strong and they stay the course to find their way back together.

I hope you enjoyed reading a tale that had personal elements woven into it. My husband and I were apart when he had to travel for many weeks without me while I wrote it, and we both felt the separation keenly as it continued longer than we had initially predicted. But how much better is life when you can look forward to being together once more!

Fortunately, in this age we have been able to FaceTime and Zoom morning, afternoon, and night, but it does make one appreciate how difficult it would have been to be apart in the time of Jane Austen with only snail mail to maintain a tenuous link to each other. The upside of my husband's extended trip is that it gave me the opportunity to write a tale of separation when I felt it most acutely.

This short novella is a companion piece to my debut novel, *The Duke Wins a Bride,* in which we discover if the generous Duke of Halmesbury can find his own happy ending after the tragic loss of his first wife.

"A sweet, touching story brought to life beautifully. It flowed very well and the voices of each character were distinct. I loved her voice. She managed to convey a range of emotions to the characters. I was completely drawn in."
- Ann Brown

"This is a beautiful second chance to love., sweet, and heartwarming. Claire Glover did an excellent job with the narration. I enjoyed it."
- Jocelyne G.

**Subscribe for your free copy of
The Captain's Wife Audiobook at
ninajarrett.com/free-audio**

ABOUT THE AUTHOR

Nina started writing her own stories in elementary school but quickly grew distracted when she finished school and moved on to non-profit work with recovering drug addicts. There she worked with people from every walk of life from privileged neighborhoods to the shanty towns of urban and rural South Africa.

One day she met a real life romantic hero. She instantly married her fellow bibliophile and moved to the USA where she enjoyed a career as a sales coaching executive at an Inc 500 company. She currently lives with her husband on the Florida Gulf Coast.

Nina believes in kindness and the indomitable power of the human spirit. She is fascinated by the amazing, funny people she has met across the world who dared to change their lives. She likes to tell mischievous tales of life-changing decisions and character transformations while drinking excellent coffee and avoiding cookies.

MORE BOOKS BY NINA JARRETT

INCONVENIENT BRIDES

Book 0 Prequels : Friends of the Duke

Book 1: The Duke Wins a Bride

Book 2: To Redeem an Earl

* * *

FRIENDS OF THE DUKE: PREQUEL ANTHOLOGY

A wealthy merchant's daughter and a struggling writer.

A missing bride and her estranged husband.

Can these gentlemen woo the ladies they desire?

Anthology: Two captivating prequel novellas full of unrequited feelings and steamy romance.

London, 1818. Dinah Honeyfield can't wait any longer. In love with her family's long-term houseguest, she's determined to get him to reveal his affections before her rich industrialist father marries her off.

Lord John Pettigrew gave up his birthright to follow his dreams. And with nothing to offer a potential wife, the aspiring author despairs he'll never be able to win the hand of the one who's been his muse.

Can they rewrite their future and plot a path to forever?

Mrs. Lydia Lewis has given up on broken promises. Marrying her soulmate only to be attacked during his heartbreaking absence, she finds refuge as an incognito ducal housekeeper.

Captain Jacob Lewis is angry and hurt. Returning from military service to discover his spouse has vanished into thin air, he begins an almost hopeless search to bring her home.

Can this star-crossed pair reclaim newlywed bliss?

Friends of the Duke is the delightful prequel anthology of the Inconvenient Brides Regency romance series. If you like worthy heroes, fast-paced plots, and enduring connections, then you'll adore Nina Jarrett's charming collection.

Buy *Friends of the Duke* for twin tales of passion today!

* * *

THE DUKE WINS A BRIDE

In this spicy historical romance, a sheltered baron's daughter and a celebrated duke agree on a marriage of convenience, but he has a secret that may ruin it all.

She is desperate to escape...

When Miss Annabel Ridley learns her betrothed has been unfaithful, she knows she must cancel the wedding. The problem is no one else seems to agree with her, least of all her father. With her wedding day approaching, she must find a way to escape her doomed marriage. She seeks out the Duke of Halmesbury to request he intercede with her rakish betrothed to break it off before the wedding day.

He is ready to try again...

Widower Philip Markham has decided it is time to search for a new wife. He hopes to find a bold bride to avoid the mistakes of his past. Fate seems to be favoring him when he finds a captivating young woman in his study begging for his help to disengage from a despised figure from his past. He astonishes her with a proposal of his own—a marriage of convenience to suit them both. If she accepts, he resolves to never reveal the truth of his past lest it ruin their chances of possibly finding love.

Can be read as a standalone book or as part of the Inconvenient Brides series of Regency romance books.

* * *

TO REDEEM AN EARL: BOOK 2

A cynical debutante and a scandalous earl find themselves entangled in an undeniable attraction. Will they open their hearts to love or will his past destroy their future together?

She has vowed she will never marry...

Miss Sophia Hayward knows all about men and their immoral behavior. She has watched her father and older brother behave like reckless fools her entire life. All she wants is to avoid marriage to a lord until she reaches her majority because she has plans which do not include a husband. Until she meets the one peer who will not take a hint.

He must have her...

Lord Richard Balfour has engaged in many disgraceful activities with the women of his past. He had no regrets until he encounters a cheeky debutante who makes him want to be a better man. Only problem is, he has a lot of bad behavior to make amends for if he is ever going to persuade Sophia to take him seriously. Will he learn to be a better man before his mistakes catch up with him and ruin their chance at true love?

Can be read as a standalone book or as part of the Inconvenient Brides series of Regency romance books.

www.ingramcontent.com/pod-product-compliance
Lightning Source LLC
Chambersburg PA
CBHW031025190726
48286CB00003BA/1024